SOULSTICE

THE DEVOURING BOOK 2

BY SIMON HOLT

LITTLE, BROWN AND COMPANY

NEW YORK   BOSTON

Also in The DEVOURING series:

The Devouring (Book 1)

Text Copyright © 2009 by Star Farm Productions, LLC

Smoke images by Yamada Taro/Riser/Getty Images, and Don Farrall/ Photographer's Choice/Getty Images.

Little, Brown and Company

Hachette Book Group
237 Park Avenue, New York, NY 10017
Visit our website at www.lb-teens.com

Little, Brown and Company is a division of Hachette Book Group, Inc.
The Little, Brown name and logo are trademarks of Hachette Book Group, Inc.

First Edition: September 2009

The characters and events portrayed in this book are fictitious. Any similarity to real persons, living or dead, is coincidental and not intended by the author.

Based upon an original idea by Mark Allen Smith.

Library of Congress Cataloging-in-Publication Data

Holt, Simon.
    Soulstice / Simon Holt.—1st ed.
        p. cm.—(The devouring ; bk. 2)
    Summary: As the summer solstice approaches, fifteen-year-old Reggie, horrified to learn that the Vours are still intent on harming her family and her best friend, Aaron, finds help from an unlikely source in discovering the secret behind the Vours' existence and ways to overcome their terrifying power.
    ISBN 978-0-316-03571-2
    [1. Fear—Fiction. 2. Supernatural—Fiction. 3. Horror stories.] I. Title.
    PZ7.H7416So 2009
    [Fic]—dc22   2008046745

10 9 8 7 6 5 4 3 2 1

Book design by Alison Impey

RRD-H

Printed in the United States of America

TO RIVER, AND TO JON.

PROLOGUE

I kept my eyes closed, smelling the buttered popcorn and cotton candy, hearing the ding-dings of the Midway games, feeling the warm sun on my skin. I breathed in and opened my eyes, smiling in readiness for the fun day ahead.

But with my eyes open I saw that the carnival was empty. The smells, the sounds were all there, but no people to enjoy it. I was standing on the platform of the Ferris wheel, and the cars rounded their wide, crayon-box arc through the sky, but there wasn't an operator tending to the ride.

The blue car was descending onto the platform, and I saw that on the seat was a rose, and tied to the rose was a card, and written on the card was my name. I dashed forward, light with glee, and grabbed up both the rose and the card. The flower was pungent, but when I opened the envelope I cut my finger on the paper, and it bled onto the ground. My finger stung, and then, to my horror, leeches crawled up through the sand and sucked up the blood. They made slurping sounds and left a trail of black sludge behind them. I felt something pinch my shoulder and cringed; one of them clung to me, its mouth suctioned to my skin, sucking my blood out of my veins. Disgusted, I swatted it away and stomped on it, but it left black crisscrosses on my arm. I examined them, but they weren't painful, so I turned back to the card.

"Meet me at the Love Boat," it read, and my heart soared. I clapped my hands in anticipation and hurried across the fairgrounds.

The Love Boat was a two-person skiff that floated down an underground river, though really the "river" was just a man-made canal built inside one of the carnival houses. But it was dark, and it was quiet, and it was perfect for kissing. And he wanted to meet me there.

The boat was waiting at the quay. It was empty, except for another note sitting on the seat.

"Set sail, I'll soon be with you," it said, so I did. I pushed off and settled in, and the boat drifted into the darkness of a steel cave.

Pink spotlights dappled off the water ahead, and the place was filled with the scent of roses. I looked over the side of the boat and saw the water filled with rose petals — he'd left them for me! I dipped my hand into the water, scooped them up, and pressed them against my nose . . .

And screamed. They were not rose petals at all, but dismembered ears, colored red with blood. My screams echoed through the cavern, but I could not go back, only forward through a listening sea.

The river rounded a bend in front of me, disappearing into the black. I called out his name, but there was no answer. The boat drifted forward, and the air grew blisteringly cold. I could see my breath, and the river began to freeze over. Fear sprouted inside me, but there was nothing I could do but float and wait for whatever was coming. I heard the noise of running water ahead, and suddenly my boat tipped, and I was shrieking and falling, falling, down an icy waterfall.

The boat crashed when it hit the waves below, but I just sank beneath them, as if I had stones tied to my ankles. Down and down I floated, the frigid water curdling my skin and freezing my organs.

Finally I reached the bottom, and there was my love, tangled in algae, his skin whiter than snow, his lips bluer than sky, his eyes opened wide and blacker than space. His dark curls wafted to and fro about his once-perfect face. He stared, unseeing, ahead, and then a crab crawled out between his lips. I tried to swim up to the surface, but he grabbed my foot and would not let go, his grip so tight it bore into my bone, and I was stuck there until the fish came to gnaw at my skin and devour my eyes.

Reggie sat up in bed, gasping for breath.

"Just the dream, just the dream," she muttered to herself. She sat still, trying to calm her breathing and push the restlessness from her body. The details of the dream sometimes varied, but the end was always the same.

She rubbed her eyes, tired and frustrated. She didn't know how to make it go away. Reaching over, she turned on her bedside lamp and took a sip of water. Her glance fell on her history notebook on the night table. Impulsively, she ripped a sheet of paper out of it, clicked open a pen, and scribbled out what she had just dreamt.

A noise in her doorway made her look up.

"Who's there?"

"It's just me," said her brother, Henry, and he stepped into the room. "I had a nightmare."

"They must be going around," Reggie replied. "Come on, hop in."

Henry dove onto her bed and snuggled with her, and soon he was fast asleep again. But Reggie lay awake long after, wondering if the nightmares would ever stop.

1

Six months, Reggie Halloway thought Friday morning as the hot water from the shower poured down her chilled flesh. Six months since Quinn Waters, town golden boy and the object of her foolish infatuation, had revealed himself as a Vour. Six months since he tried to destroy her and later drowned in Cutter's Lake while Reggie's psyche battled for Henry's soul inside the fearscape.

Six months since she'd encountered a Vour at all.

The monsters were the essence of fear, and they took over people's bodies on Sorry Night, the night of the winter solstice. They sent human souls to personal hells called fearscapes and lived out the lives their victims should have had. Reggie had first read about the Vours in an old journal, stories of ancient and evil creatures who saw human beings either as hosts to their essences or playthings to torment. She had thought them the delusions of a madwoman, Macie Canfield, but then one had gotten to Reggie's brother. She had learned how to defeat it and had brought her brother back.

At first she had suspected every person on the street of being a Vour, scoured every feature and action for the telltale signs.

Vours blended in seamlessly, with few giveaways. They hated the cold and couldn't cry, and would sometimes manifest as smoke when they were injured or leaving a body. Or when they telepathically sent horrific visions to other humans, which they often did just for fun. But she had seen nothing, not since January.

Perhaps they'd decided to leave her alone. Perhaps her fluke power to enter and destroy the hellish fearscape had shown them something they'd never encountered. Perhaps *she* had scared *them* away.

"Come on, Reg!" Dad rapped on the bathroom door. "Let's move it. Out the door in ten!"

"Almost done!"

She rinsed the conditioner out of her hair. It hung just below her chin now; she had had to cut much of it off after she'd singed it away in Macie's burning basement. But it was growing back, healthy, strong, and curiously, a shade darker.

It wasn't the only thing that was darker, Reggie mused. A slow dread continued to creep like black moss across the heart of Cutter's Wedge, and the town remained on edge.

Quinn Waters was seventeen and Cutter's Wedge's favorite son. The dimpled boy next door and the star quarterback since his sophomore year, he passed and ran a primrose path to Division A ball. His academic record wasn't stellar, but it would have been strong enough to earn options and scholarships to top programs around the country. No one suspected what he really was. How could they? He was perfect. Charismatic, charming, gentlemanly, and seriously cute, Quinn had everyone under his spell. And then he had disappeared.

Though few spoke it aloud, most of the town believed that their young hero had met with foul play. And no one would rest until answers — and a body — were unearthed. Reggie, along with her best friend, Aaron Cole, and former mentor, Eben Bloch, knew the boy's body was at the bottom of the lake, but this was a dark secret all three planned to take to their graves.

A homicide detective from Wennemack had descended on Cutter's Wedge in late February, two months after the disappearance, and had been lurking around ever since. After four months of investigation, which involved dozens of interviews with students and faculty at Cutter High, the detective and the local police had made little progress, and neither Quinn nor his red Mustang had been found. In all that time, nobody had ever interviewed Reggie or Aaron.

And why would they? Reggie had often asked herself. She and Aaron hadn't exactly traveled in Quinn's circle. Nothing connected them to Quinn. Nothing except that car . . .

"Reggie!" Dad's voice now boomed from the kitchen below. "Let's go!"

Reggie pulled on her army-green Chucks, already tied, and jogged down the stairs dressed in jeans and a plain white tee. Henry stood at the front door, a faded red cap pulled down over his ears.

"Might hit ninety-five today." Reggie gently patted him on the head. "Little hot for that, don't you think?"

Henry shrugged.

"If anyone says anything, you tell them —"

"I tell them I lost my ear in a tragic circus accident involving a mountain lion and a renegade trapeze artist, I know," Henry said. "It doesn't help, Reggie."

"Henry, screw Billy Persons and anyone else that stupid. If he teases you again, you tell him his mother is a raging alcoholic."

"You will say no such thing." Dad emerged from the kitchen, his tool belt slung over his shoulder. "Henry, do me a favor and grab the paper from the end of the driveway?"

"Can't you just get it on your way to work?"

"Henry."

"Fine."

The boy stomped out of the front door. Thom Halloway dropped a heavy, calloused palm on his daughter's shoulder.

"Reggie."

"What."

"Don't be reckless. Not with him. Please."

Reggie shook off her father's hand.

"I'm trying to help."

"By encouraging him to slur another kid's mother?"

"By helping him fight back, Dad!"

"That's not your job. Let the doctor do the helping."

"Yeah." Reggie walked out toward the street.

"Reggie, I'm not —"

"Have a nice day, Dad."

Reggie and Henry met up with Aaron two blocks from the unified school campus. At fifteen, Aaron had sprouted up several inches in the past year, and his gawky stride suggested that his body didn't quite know how to handle the spurt. His large hands and feet, coupled with a T-shirt and cords that hung from his thin frame, gave him the look of a puppy still growing into its skin.

It was already hot and sticky, and the promise of another sweltering day rose from the asphalt. Heavy spring rains had caused flooding around the county and a lot of standing water remained. Mosquitoes staked an early claim to ponds and puddles all over town on a relentless search for blood.

"Last week before finals, Reg. You ready?"

"Not even close."

Henry walked ahead, jumping over sidewalk cracks, the red cap still tugged over his ears. Aaron saw the expression of concern on Reggie's face but did not ask.

"So." Aaron smacked a mosquito on his neck. "Bio."

"Ugh. Don't."

"Let's hear it. Wasp. Phylum?"

Reggie sighed. "Phylum arthropod. Subphylum myriapod. Class insect."

"Close. Subphylum *hexapod*."

"Damn."

"You'll do fine." Aaron slapped another bug off his arm.

"I've resigned myself to the sea of mediocrity that is the 3.6 GPA. Enjoy the thin air of your 4.0 peak."

"4.2, actually. You know, with the weighted classes." Aaron paused, embarrassed. "I'll stop now."

"No, don't. You should be proud. Besides, plenty of people have lived happy, fruitful lives thinking a hexapod is a curse on peas, right?"

"This is a fact."

They reached the corner of the block, and Henry stopped on the edge of the vast elementary school lawn. He gazed out at the gaggle of small children playing in front of the main entrance to Cutter's Wedge Elementary. There was yelling and laughter, but something kept Henry from joining in the fun. Something other than the worries about his ear. Reggie eyed him — it had been like this since he'd come back from the fearscape.

Reggie knelt down and gave him a little squeeze.

"You have a good day, okay, Hen? Go play."

Henry's frame went rigid. Reggie looked up and saw a hefty, carrot-haired boy chasing a couple of smaller boys. He tackled one of them and pinned him down.

It didn't look like play to Reggie.

"I want to break his legs so he can't do that," Henry said in a low voice.

Reggie pulled away, startled.

"You don't mean that. Look, Billy Persons is a chubby snot-nosed brat."

Aaron leaned in. "And he smells like cabbage. Just like his big brother."

Henry let out a little laugh.

Reggie squeezed harder. "You won't let him get to you, right?"

"Yeah." Henry kicked at the ground. "Is Dad picking me up?"

"No, he's at a Wennemack site on Fridays for a while. That's why you had your appointment yesterday, remember?" Reggie stroked her brother's hand. "But I'll be right here after school."

Henry hugged her. "See you."

"See you."

Reggie watched him walk into the schoolyard. Then she and Aaron headed across the drive that separated the elementary school from Cutter High.

"How are his sessions with Dr. Unger going?" Aaron asked.

"Pretty well, I think. I haven't met him yet, but Henry likes him, anyway."

So far, Henry hadn't remembered anything about being taken over by a Vour, or about spending several hellish days in his fearscape. But he had been having terrible nightmares since March, which Dad and the doctors chalked up to stress from Mom leaving, hence the weekly therapy sessions.

"Good. Unger is the best child trauma therapist in the state. My mom swears by him. He'll help Henry get better, Reggie. And he *will* get better."

"I know." Reggie breathed deep and ran her fingers through her hair. "So, just one more week, right?"

"Yep. One more week, and then we can spend our days lying by the pool sipping lemonade. You know, if one of us had a pool."

"And if I didn't need a job."

"There might be work at the bookstore. I can ask Eben —"

"No," Reggie said flatly. She hadn't seen Eben Bloch since January when she'd quit her job at his shop and Aaron had taken over.

"Reg, you know Eben isn't exactly the Dr. Phil sharing type. But I can tell he misses you. I think he feels like he's lost a daughter. You're his only family."

"Families don't lie to each other."

"Really? You haven't been straight with your dad about what happened. Not that I blame you. He'd put you away. But Eben has his reasons why he didn't tell you he had a history with the Vours. He was trying to protect you."

Reggie wiped sweat from her brow.

"Remind me again how *not* telling me pertinent information is protecting me."

They headed across the quad. Normally, students would chat under trees or up against the bike racks until the last possible moment, but the oppressive humidity had driven even the laziest kids into the building prior to the bell. Reggie noticed a patrol car and a black sedan with tinted windows in the parking lot.

"Cops again," she said. "When will they stop?"

"When Quinn's case goes cold." Aaron opened the door for Reggie and glanced nervously at the vehicles. "Or when they make an arrest."

They both stepped into the school entrance hall as distant thunder rumbled in the darkening sky.

2

Reggie slid into her English class desk, her back and neck already sweaty and gross. She pulled her damp ponytail up again, but the rubber band snapped and her hair unraveled in a mess of frizz.

The rest of the students filed into the classroom as the bell sounded. Despite the continued presence of police at the school, there was an air of excitement. Kids chatted and laughed as if, for at least a little while, they'd moved past the anxiety and gloom brought on by Quinn's bizarre and sudden disappearance. Summer vacation was almost here, and everyone felt it.

Nina Snow, perfectly coiffed and confident as usual, took her seat behind Reggie. Her hair was long, dark, and frizz-less, her skin clear like porcelain. She looked like the only girl in school unaffected by the heat. The one freshman to be recruited for varsity cheerleading at Cutter, Nina had been Quinn's girlfriend since Homecoming. She ignored most of her female freshmen classmates, but Reggie had unwittingly drawn her attention last December when Nina had noticed Quinn flirting with her.

"Bride of Frankenstein," Nina said. "Not a good look for you. Then, do you *have* a good look?"

Reggie said nothing.

"What, no witty comeback from the literary loser?"

Mercifully, Mr. Machen strolled in.

"Okay, monkeys. Simmer down."

A few students screeched and scratched their heads and armpits. Machen smirked and shook his head.

"I'm still your zookeeper for another week."

Machen was Reggie's favorite teacher — an extended substitute who'd taken over Honors English some months earlier, after Mrs. Harter had fortuitously been offered a grant to study the works of nineteenth-century playwrights in London. Machen, in his mid-thirties but with hair so blond it looked almost white, was passionate about literature, and was equally well-versed in mythology and history. He wore tweed jackets that made him look the standard scattered professor type, but Reggie quickly learned he was impeccably organized and methodical.

"Mr. M, what's on the final?"

"Two essays. No less than four *full* pages a pop. And no, you cannot use crayon, write in all capital letters, or double-space."

The class groaned.

"You'll need to prep for three. Unless you want to roll the dice. I advise against that. Questions?"

Nina raised her hand.

"Miss Snow."

"Can we at least get one topic ahead of time?"

"Where's the sport in that?"

The class begged as one chorus.

"Fine. Obviously, one of the essays will be on *Midsummer*. Which you *all* finished this week as assigned, right?"

Machen raised an eyebrow as students quietly pulled out their dog-eared copies of Shakespeare's *A Midsummer Night's Dream*.

"Appropriate that exams are just a week before midsummer. The solstice. What's this time of year about? Anyone? Mr. Cole."

Even though Honors sections had the brightest and most diligent kids, Aaron was always the best bet to open classroom discussions. It was safe to assume he'd not only read the play, but then reread it, cross-referenced the annotations, and probably joined an online chat group called "Buds of the Bard" or something equally nerdy.

"Um. Solstice. Derived from the Latin, meaning 'sun standing still.' The longest day of the year when the tilt of the Earth's axis is oriented directly toward the Sun so the light reaches its southernmost extremes. The opposite is true on the winter solstice, when the least amount of light . . ."

Reggie could see eyes rolling all around Aaron. She jumped in.

"It's also a time of magic, right? Represented by the land of Faerie in the play."

"Yes. Magic. Mystery. Mischief. All of these things play out in Shakespeare's best comedy on the longest day of the year." Machen nodded at Reggie. "But the summer solstice also represents rebirth. An awakening."

He went on, pacing enthusiastically and quoting Nick Bottom's singing spell upon the sleeping faerie queen, Titania. The class breathed a collective sigh, knowing that once Machen was on a roll, he'd be unlikely to stop to ask questions that would prove most of them hadn't finished the play.

Reggie tried to focus, but activity outside the classroom windows diverted her attention. Across the street, a small group of children played on the elementary school jungle gym. A thick bed of charcoal gray clouds had swallowed up the morning, and a strong wind blew weeds and scraps of paper across the quad lawn. No competent teacher would have taken kids out in such menacing weather. Plus school had just started for the day. The first large droplets of rain pattered on the plate-glass windows.

Reggie turned back to the teacher, who continued to pace and gesture dramatically with his free hand, but his words washed over Reggie like a dull tide. She looked out the window again and saw a little boy with a red cap on his head.

Henry.

Another larger boy chased him around the jungle gym.

"Miss Halloway. Continue from where I left off?"

"I . . ." Reggie panicked, unsure where they were in the text.

"Are you with us?"

"Yes, but . . ." Reggie fumbled with her book and it dropped to the floor. She reached down to pick it up.

"Miss Snow. Continue please."

The rain fell harder now. Lightning arced and thunder boomed in the distance. Reggie jumped in her seat, but the rest of her class seemed not to notice the rapidly threatening storm.

"I see their knavery: this is to make an ass of me; to fright me, if they could . . ."

Outside, the kids pranced around the playground, hopping in puddles and swooshing down wet slides. They all laughed and played except for two of them.

Billy Persons had Henry pinned down in the mud. No adults appeared to be outside with the children.

"... but I will not stir from this place, do what they can: I will walk up and down here, and I will sing, that they shall hear I am not afraid..."

Reggie leaped to her feet.

"Henry!"

Nina stopped reciting. The whole class turned to Reggie.

"Miss Halloway. Is everything all right?"

Shock and embarrassment flooded through her.

"I..."

She looked out the window again. The children were gone. Henry and Billy, gone. Reggie sat back down, her breath short and panicky. What was going on?

"Miss Halloway. Why don't you pick it up for us from here? Read Bottom's response to Titania's irrational profession of love."

"I..."

"Middle of page thirty-six. Line twenty-four."

Reggie fumbled to the page and scanned the text with a shaking finger.

"Methinks, mistress, you should have little reason for that: and yet, to say the truth, reason and love keep little company together now-a-days..."

"What is Bottom saying to the faerie queen here?"

Reggie looked outside again and let out a startled gasp. Henry stood just outside her classroom window, his forehead pressed to the glass. His eyes, dark and menacing, bore into her. Rain cascaded down his face, ugly streaks of gray water pouring from his nose.

He held something in his hand.

"Henry . . ."

The boy slowly lifted up a severed ear and pressed it against the windowpane. Blood dribbled out of it and down the glass.

Reggie screamed and dove from her chair toward the window. She tripped over Nina's bag and fell to the floor.

"Aren't you proud of me, Reggie?" Henry's voice was hollow, and his lips parted in a mirthless smile, revealing gray teeth and black gums. "I stood up for myself. Isn't that what you wanted?"

Behind him the trees were blown horizontal in the thrashing wind. The rain pounded down and froze into streaks of crystallized ice on his face. Dark smoke poured from his nose and mouth, rising and whirling into the air in a cyclone.

Then it surged toward the window.

Reggie covered her face as the glass exploded. It blew her back onto the floor, and she could feel the shards sticking into her arms and cheeks. Pain shot through her skin, and she knew her blood was dripping, pooling, mingling with the rain blowing in from outside.

She screamed and screamed and screamed.

"Reggie! Reggie, stop!"

She could hear voices, but at first they were too muffled to make out. Reggie had a vague notion she was lying down; the floor beneath her felt cool.

"I'm here. You're okay. It's me."

She stopped screaming and focused on a familiar voice.

Aaron.

"Can you hear me? Come back."

She felt his touch on her cheeks and forehead. He cradled her head and brushed the hair out of her face.

"I'm with you. You're safe."

Aaron's face came into focus. It was creased with worry.

Reggie's eyes darted about, taking in the horrified faces of the classmates that surrounded her.

Aaron looked up. "Can you guys give her some room?"

"Everyone, please." Machen cleared the students away. His voice shook. "Let her breathe."

"Are you back?" Aaron asked.

Reggie managed a nod and tried to sit up. Machen squatted down beside them.

"I'll call the nurse, Reggie. Stay still."

"No, it's okay. Aaron will take me."

Machen acquiesced, and he and Aaron helped Reggie to her feet. Her best friend held her close as he walked her toward the door.

"My stuff."

"Don't worry. I'll grab it later. Come on."

Nervous whispers and snickers trailed behind them. The whole class had watched in stunned silence as Reggie had leaped from her seat and pounded her fists against the window. She'd struck it so hard that one of the massive panes had splintered into a web of glass. Then she'd fallen to the ground, flailing and screaming at absolutely nothing. Reggie guessed what they were thinking: had their classmate lost her mind?

There were more students in the hallway than normal as Aaron escorted a shaking Reggie toward the parking lot exit of the school. All of them should have been in class, prepping for final exams or making up missed work. But something was wrong, and news about Reggie's episode could not have reached the rest of the school so quickly.

Pockets of nervous students huddled near lockers, murmuring to one another. Snatches of conversation reached Reggie's ears.

". . . Quinn . . ."

". . . found it in a lake . . ."

". . . a body?"

". . . no, car . . ."

Aaron pulled Reggie closer to him.

"Keep walking, Reggie. Come on."

As they neared the exit, a set of heels clacked behind them, moving at a steady but fast clip.

"Aaron Cole."

Aaron and Reggie froze.

"Mr. Cole, please remove your hands from the young lady and put them on top of your head."

Both Reggie and Aaron spun around to face a detective from Wennemack Homicide. Two Cutter's Wedge patrolmen stood on either side of her, and one of them had a pair of handcuffs opened.

"Young lady, step away from him now, please."

Reggie just gaped at her, but Aaron instinctively took a step backward.

"Do not move," the detective said to him with an eerie calm. "We do not want an incident."

"What's happening?" Aaron's voice wavered.

"Aaron Cole, you are being detained for questioning in the disappearance of Quinn Waters."

"What?"

One of the patrolman grabbed Aaron away from Reggie and pulled him toward the front entrance of the school. The rest of the students in the hall watched in silent shock.

"You can't do that!" Reggie said, but the detective stalked past, ignoring her.

"Please follow my instructions," she said. "You will have the right to contact an attorney from the Wennemack station, but right now I urge you to cooperate."

Aaron craned his neck backward.

"Reggie?"

The patrolman put a meaty hand on Aaron's head and twisted it forward. The detective trailed behind the two men and Aaron as they led him out the door. Reggie started to follow, but the school nurse stepped in front of her. Mrs. Hoppins wrung her hands anxiously.

"Reggie, I need to speak with you."

"Mrs. Hoppins, please . . ."

"It's your little brother. Something's happened. Your father is on his way . . ."

"What is it? Is he at the school?"

"Yes, but come with me, we —"

But Reggie was already out the side exit and running across the parking lot toward the elementary school playground.

3

The scissors pressed up against the soft doughy skin of the larger boy's throat. Mucus and blood poured from his nose and dripped onto Henry's hand, but the smaller boy seemed not to notice. Billy, beaten and exhausted, slumped awkwardly on the ground, legs splayed and head twisted upward. He had stopped crying and now whimpered in steady intervals. Henry crouched behind him with his pale and thin left arm wrapped around Billy's neck just above the scissor points. The playground smelled of wet wood chips and rubber tires. Behind them, faces peered out of the elementary school windows, students staring in wide-eyed fascination at the tense scene outside. Some had begun to cry.

"Henry?" Dr. Heath, the school principal, inched forward, her manicured hands extended in an unthreatening manner. "Henry? Listen to me. Nobody's going to hurt you. Let go of Billy."

"Please, honey," Miss Richards, Henry's third grade teacher, pleaded. "You don't want to hurt anyone. You're a good boy."

"No, I'm not."

"Henry!" Reggie shouted as she raced across the thick lawn toward her brother. "Let him go!"

"I told you to leave me alone," Henry said again, this time in a whisper audible only to Billy. "Why couldn't you just leave me alone?"

"Henry." Reggie stopped ten yards away and just stared. Was this really happening, or was it another vision? "What are you doing?"

Henry's hand trembled; the scissor points quivered against Billy's exposed skin. He looked pleadingly at his sister.

"What *am* I, Reggie?"

Reggie approached him slowly and knelt on the ground a few feet away. Billy wailed and clutched Henry's red cap tightly in his fist. Henry's deformed ear, almost lost completely from frostbite the night on the lake, was exposed for everyone to see.

"You're my brother. You're Henry." She inched forward on her knees. "You're just my Henry."

"I see things, Reggie." The scissors shook in his small hand. "I close my eyes and I see awful things."

Tears welled in Reggie's eyes. She fought to keep them back. "I know. I see them, too."

"You do?"

"Yes."

"Can you make them stop?"

The principal took small and cautious steps toward them.

"I'm going to try." Slowly, Reggie reached out her hand and laid it gently on Henry's arm. "I know you don't want to hurt anyone. Now let him go."

Henry sobbed and dropped the scissors. Billy jerked his head free and scrambled across the wood chips on hands and knees. Dr. Heath scooped him up like an infant and raced him into the building, just as a patrol car zoomed onto the grass with lights flashing and spinning. Thom Halloway's old pickup followed. Miss Richards ran to address the first police officer as he jumped out of his car, a hand on his holstered sidearm.

Reggie ignored the noise and hugged Henry tightly. He whimpered into her shoulder.

"What happened to me?"

"I'm so sorry, Hen. This is my fault. I should have told you."

"Told me what?"

Thom Halloway raced across the playground but stopped several feet short of his two children.

"Reggie?"

"Take us home, Dad."

"What the hell is going on? Henry —?"

"Dad. Please. Take us home."

But the Halloway family didn't pull into their driveway for another several hours. After such a disturbing incident, the Cutter's Wedge police chief, the emergency medical team on the scene, and the school district's superintendent demanded that Henry be evaluated before being released to his father's care.

Dr. Heath sent the rest of the students home for the day, and Dr. Unger, the child psychologist from the Thornwood

Psychiatric Hospital who had been treating Henry for the past two months, was summoned to the elementary school. It was near dark before he cleared Henry to go home with his father and sister — provided that the entire family commit to immediate and intense group sessions together starting the following day. Even so, the police chief said the DA's office would be deciding over the next few days whether to officially charge Henry with criminal assault and battery.

And though there was now less than a week left before summer vacation, the superintendent had little choice but to expel Henry. The boy would need a clean psychological evaluation before the district board could consider reinstating him in the town public school system.

The adults did not discuss the wider and possibly more damaging repercussions of the day. Nobody spoke aloud of lawsuits, but Reggie suspected her father would contact his attorney first thing in the morning. He had already announced they'd be leaving at 9:30 to go to Thornwood for their first family therapy session.

On the silent and tense drive home, she fought off thoughts of all the distress that Henry's violent attack on Billy Persons would bring to her family, especially in light of the events from December and her own breakdown in the middle of class the same day. The high school would probably be phoning Dad tomorrow to report that incident. Wonderful.

Dad carried a sleepy Henry into the house, and Reggie followed, locking up behind them. Dad turned to her.

"I want you to stay here while I take Henry up to bed."

"I'll take him, Dad."

"No, I want you to —"

"Dad?" Henry lifted his head off his father's shoulder. "I'm sorry about today. I know you're mad."

"I'm not mad at you, little man."

"If I'm the one who caused all the trouble, why are you upset with Reggie? "

"I'm not . . ." Dad scratched his scruffy chin. "It's complicated, Henry. Reggie and I just need to talk."

Henry twisted his body and held his arms out to Reggie. Dad reluctantly let her take him.

"Holy cow, you're heavy."

Dad kissed Henry on the forehead, then put his hand on Reggie's shoulder.

"Come down right after."

"Yes, sir."

Reggie carried Henry up to his room and lowered him onto his bed. He slid under the sheets and pulled them up over his chest. Reggie sat down next to him.

"Henry, what happened today?"

Henry lowered his head onto the pillow and closed his eyes. He took a slow, deep breath and opened them again.

"I'm starting to remember things. Terrible things."

Henry's eyes seemed to sink back a little in his head, and they took on a faraway gaze. Reggie noticed how old and dark they appeared now. No longer young and innocent.

"A carnival. And a shooting game with heads. And a clown. The one from that movie I watched, the one with the hatchet for a hand."

"Yes."

"And a hospital with demon babies and ghosts of dead children."

"Yes."

"And Mom."

"No, Henry. That wasn't really Mom."

"But it looked like her. And it talked like her."

"But it wasn't her."

"It was the monster. The monster inside me."

"Yes." Reggie brushed Henry's mussed hair from his face. "But the monster is gone now."

"You killed it."

"No, you did."

"Me?"

"Yes."

"But you were there with me."

"Yes."

"And you helped me."

"All I did was help you find the strength you had all along. You had all the power you ever needed to destroy the monster inside you. I just reminded you of that."

Henry glanced across the room at the empty hamster cage.

"During our spelling quiz today, Otto, our class hamster, was running on his wheel. And I was concentrating so hard, and the wheel was squeaking and squeaking, and then I just remembered." He blinked. "General Squeak. He didn't run away like you said, did he?"

"No. He didn't run away."

"I killed him." Henry held his hands in front of his face and stared at them. "It feels like a dream because I was in that other place. But I remember. I can see it happening. I killed him with my own hands. I heard his bones snap."

Reggie took her brother's hands in her own. "No. The monster did it. It did it because it was cruel, because it hated the things you loved." Reggie took a breath. "The monster that was inside you — it was a Vour. Like from the book I read you. They were real, and I was stupid enough to let one get to you. I'm so sorry, Henry, so sorry."

They both cried, and seeing Henry's tears relieved Reggie. She was sad, but heartened. Tears were human and a Vour could never cry.

"I didn't want to hurt him. Billy."

"I know."

"I had all these awful things in my head, and then on the playground he said I was weird and creepy, and everyone was scared of me, and he called me a freak. And then, it was like, I knew he was right. I *am* a freak — a monster. I just wanted him to stop, I didn't want him to tell anyone."

"But it wasn't you!"

Henry had stopped crying, and now he stared straight ahead, thoughtful and unseeing.

"Sometimes I feel it. Like it's in me. It isn't in my mind anymore, but still . . ."

"The monster is gone. I watched it die." Reggie wiped her eyes. "You loved Squeak," she said. "You love Dad. And you love Mom, even though she hurt us and left us to grow up without her. You *love*, Henry. That is something a Vour can't ever do."

Henry's eyes closed, and his breathing became quiet and calm. Reggie stayed close to him and listened as he drifted off to sleep.

"I love you, Reggie."

"I love you, too."

She kissed his forehead, then walked to the door and shut off the light. As she looked back at him lying peacefully in bed, she thought of her vision from the morning and began to tremble. Yes, she had watched the monster die, or so she thought, but she was still afraid that the Vour was somewhere inside her brother, lurking, waiting to take him back.

4

The interrogation room wasn't like the ones Aaron had seen so many times on his mom's favorite crime shows. There was no mirrored pane of one-way glass. No good cop teamed up with a bad cop to break him down. He sat alone in a gray room, listening to a leaky pipe drip incessantly from the ceiling behind him. A tripod-mounted camcorder stood watch from across the table.

Occasionally, the woman who had brought him in peered through the door's barred window. She was taller than average and thin, with blond hair pulled back into a ponytail. She wore a black suit and sharp-heeled boots that clicked on the tiled floor when she walked. She was stylish, and she was badass, but her skin was almost gray, and every one of her facial features was pointy and grim; when she looked at Aaron, he was reminded of an eagle searching for prey.

On the ride in from Cutter's Wedge, she'd told him that her name was Detective Gale, and she was taking him to the police station in Wennemack — but that was all. She ignored him when he asked for his parents.

They'd kept him here by himself, in an isolated part of the precinct, for what seemed like hours. Aaron worked silently through scenarios in his head and tried to stay calm.

If Quinn's body had been found, surely he'd know by now. But with only circumstantial evidence, it was unlikely that any formal charge would be filed against him. He used this knowledge to keep panic at bay. And one crucial fact comforted him in this mess: the police had not brought Reggie in with him. Aaron planned to keep her out of it.

Drip. Drip. Drip went the leak behind him.

Finally, the door squeaked open and Detective Gale walked in. She set down her briefcase and clicked on the camcorder. A red light flashed as she trained the lens on Aaron.

"I have some questions for you," Gale said.

"Where are my parents? And I want a lawyer."

"We're just talking here. Relax. You'll get your phone call when we're done. How well did you know Quinn Waters?"

"Not very," Aaron replied. "Superstar. Geek. Our species don't really mix."

"But you did favors for him, right? Wrote his term papers?"

Aaron grimaced. Someone had ratted him out.

"Is that why you brought me in?"

"Answer the question."

"I helped him out sometimes . . . like a tutor."

"But he paid you. You wrote the papers, he turned them in with his name on them. You had a scam going."

"No, it wasn't like that —"

Gale interrupted and folded her hands in front of her.

"You're a smart kid. Top of your class, attentive at school, on your way to a great college. But you have another side to you, don't you?"

"I don't get what you mean."

"Your parents. Your teachers. They see the Aaron Cole who gets straight A's, takes all the hardest classes, is a member of the Quiz Bowl team. The good kid," Gale said. "But then there's this other Aaron Cole. The sneaky one. The dishonest one."

"Are you trying to scare me with this?"

"The one with a morbid fantasy life."

"What? No, that's just a hobby —"

Gale leaned forward.

"Paging through books like *A History of Demonic Possession* and *The Encyclopedia of Serial Killers* is a hobby?"

Aaron squirmed in his seat but said nothing.

Detective Gale opened her briefcase and took out a manila folder. She arranged a series of photographs from it in front of Aaron. They depicted a red Mustang being hauled from a lake. In addition to damage probably caused by being sunk under water for a long period of time, the entire back end was smashed in.

"Do you know what this is?" she asked.

"It looks like it could be Quinn's car." Aaron tried to keep his voice calm, but it cracked anyway. "Can I get some water or something?"

"In a minute. We pulled it from one of the chain lakes up near Fredericks. Based on plant life growth found in the car, my investigators think it was submerged for about six months," Gale said. "How about that? Six months. Right around the time Quinn disappeared."

"I don't know anything about it."

"Most of the time, when a car's been in the water that long, all trace evidence is gone. But sometimes we get lucky."

Gale paused and crossed her hands in front of her, waiting for a reaction from Aaron. He hoped that he gave none.

She went on. "We know something big and heavy took out the back of this car, like an SUV. So we compared the size and shapes of the dents in the Mustang to every other SUV in this county. And we came up with an exact match. What's more, there were paint scrapings on the fender. Just trace amounts, but enough to analyze. GMC Silvercube. And of all the students who attend Cutter High, only one family has this particular GMC SUV, in this particular color." Gale smiled. "Guess whose?"

That was it. The blow he'd been hoping wouldn't come. He didn't need to guess.

"I want to call my parents."

"What happened, Aaron? Did Quinn promise you something besides money in exchange for papers? Status? Popularity? Did he fail to deliver?"

"It was not like that at all," said Aaron. "And I think I'm done answering questions."

"Did he go back on his promises? Keep ignoring you in the hall? Rag on you? Maybe you just couldn't take it anymore."

"I want my phone call."

"We've called your parents already. They're on their way, but the roads are a mess because of the storm. There's a flash flood warning, too." Gale gestured to the ceiling, where water dripped from a few more places. "See for yourself. This place is leaking like a sieve."

Aaron's trepidation turned to anger.

"I'm a *minor*. You can't do this. You're trying to pin something on me, but I'm not going to give you what you want."

"I think you will."

Gale stuck a hand in her jacket pocket and pulled out a pair of latex gloves. She put them on, then reached into the briefcase beside her and drew out a pocketknife in a plastic evidence bag. She took the knife out of the bag, and with a snap of her wrist, the blade clacked open. Aaron chilled.

"We found this out at Cutter's Lake."

Gale held the same knife he'd taken from the glove box of his mother's car and used to slash Quinn's feet; two quick cuts that had reddened the snow with blood and prevented the Vour from chasing after Reggie.

Water dripped from the ceiling all around, faster now and more steadily.

"His blood was found in the hinge joint of this knife, Aaron. He must have been cut up pretty bad." She set it down on the table, pointing toward him. "It will go better for you if you confess now. The DA is willing to cut a deal. No one wants to see a promising kid like you go down for Murder One."

The words struck him like an ax. Murder One. Aaron looked away from Gale, feeling the camera's cold stare and the detective's probing eyes bear down on him.

Her voice dropped to a wicked purr. "If we find your DNA on

this, there's nothing more I can do for you. I'll give you a few minutes to consider."

Gale stood and left the room. The camcorder stayed on, red light flashing. Aaron sat back in his chair, shaking. His mouth was dry, and only made worse by the incessant *drip drip drip* behind him. It echoed in his head, louder now, like a stampede of thoughts. *Murder. Guilty. Prison.*

The knife shone dully on the table. Maybe Gale wanted him to attempt something crazy. Maybe she just wanted him to put his fingerprints on the knife. He wasn't sure of anything anymore.

Something touched his hair. He looked up, and a fat drop fell and splashed onto his forehead. The leak had spread across the entire ceiling, the water stain creeping across it like a morphing Rorschach test. Droplets showered onto the table and tiles, kicking up spray as they landed. Soon the photographs of Quinn's Mustang were soaked through, and they began to warp and bend.

Aaron glanced about, confused. Water now streamed down the walls all around him, collecting in pools on the floor. Then he felt the room shake, like an earthquake had hit. Aaron leaped out of his seat.

"What's going on?" he called out.

Streams of red trickled from the knife and oozed across the tabletop, the dried blood mixing with the water. With no drainage in the room, the water level rose quickly, and soon it sloshed around Aaron's shins. It was brown and dirty with the rust from the pipes, and it smelled of mold and iron. He splashed over to the door and started pounding on it.

"There's a flood! Hey! Let me out of here!"

Aaron heard the sound of creaking metal, and a pipe in the ceiling above him exploded, bursting a hole in the drywall. Dark water gushed through the gap, and he pressed himself against the wall. Horror ripped through him at the sight of the filth now up to his thighs.

Just beneath the surface, it surged and undulated with life. He felt something whip around his legs, and his knees nearly buckled. He thought he saw red eyes glowing in the murky water. The creature surfaced: it was a rat the size of Aaron's shin. Its fur was slick and greasy, its teeth like daggers, and it padded at the water with sharp claws. It swam around Aaron once, then disappeared beneath the surface again.

The water was above his waist. Waves moved through the interrogation room, and more rats plopped down from the broken pipes. Aaron felt them bump against him, their small paws clawing at him. He tried to kick them away, but then a stab of pain shot through him as a pair of fangs bit into his thigh. He screamed.

The camcorder buzzed and shorted out. Aaron tried to regain control of his mind and push the terrors away, but the teeth continued to tear at his legs, his arms, his chest. He shrieked until the flood reached his mouth, the water rank with his own blood, drowning him in a sea of hell . . .

<hr />

The digital camcorder relayed the feed from the interrogation room to the station's security control center. A few officers stood around, observing the Cutter High boy's disturbing behavior. Minutes earlier he had begun pounding on the door and clawing at the walls, shouting about a flood and drowning and rats. But the only water was just a tiny leak in the corner.

"Guess he's going for the insanity defense," said one officer, taking a sip of coffee.

"The kid is truly screwy," said another. "Gale's going to have her hands full with that nutjob."

They all nodded, but none of them noticed that, in the corner of the screen, the video showed Detective Gale standing behind the reinforced window. A smile played about her otherwise dull and dead-looking face as she gazed intently at Aaron, watching his descent into madness.

But Aaron noticed. Before the sludge engulfed him completely, before he drowned in water that wasn't there, he glimpsed her through the glass and saw a wisp of smoke drift from her nostrils.

5

Dad mixed his scotch and soda, the ice cubes clinking softly against the glass as Reggie walked into his office.

"He loves you more than anything," Dad said without turning around. "That boy's heart is so big I almost can't bear it. But I don't know how to help him."

"You're doing your best."

Dad took a sip of his drink. "Am I?" He walked over to the weathered brown leather couch and sat down. He looked worn. "I'm not so sure."

Reggie stood in the doorway, awkward and uneasy. She'd witnessed her father when he was furious, even irrational. And as much as those moments upset her, nothing made her as nervous as when he appeared lost.

"He almost cut a boy today." Dad took another drink and rubbed his eyes. "Where does the violence come from? I've never raised a hand to either of you."

"I know."

"But just now? He seemed so sweet. Is it an act? Is my son turning into some kind of monster?"

Six months ago, the Vour had quietly violated the sanctity of their home. It slept under their roof. It ate their food. It assumed its dark and evil place inside an innocent little boy. Then slowly it tried to rip apart their fragile lives.

And Thom Halloway had never suspected a thing.

"No, Dad. He's not a monster."

"Then what's happening to him, Reggie?"

Reggie moved to the swivel chair next to her father's drafting table and sat down.

"He's a good kid. He just needs our love and support. He's been through so much. First Mom. And then the accident."

Dad looked at Reggie, his eyes fixed with hers.

"The accident."

His shift in tone sent shivers through her.

"We've never talked about what happened that night."

"You know what happened."

"No. I don't. I know what you told me. But I could never make sense of it. Not really. Reggie, your brother lost part of his ear to hypothermia. What the hell were you doing out there on the lake?"

Reggie squirmed in her seat.

Throwing my possessed little brother into freezing water to make the Vour inside him weak enough for me to enter his fearscape. Naturally. What else would we be doing?

"We were skating," she said. "I told you."

Thom Halloway sat forward in the couch, his large, strong hands pressed against his knees with enough force to make the knuckles turn white.

"Bullshit."

The response caught Reggie off guard, and she instinctively pushed herself away from her father on the wheeled chair.

"Stop lying to me."

"I'm not lying!"

Her father got up and stood over her.

"I can see it in your face, Reggie!"

Reggie jumped to her feet. She wanted to hold her ground against her father, but she felt so small next to him.

"It was an accident! That's all. A stupid mistake. We never should have been out there, I know, but —"

"Was it some kind of suicide pact?"

"What?"

"You and Aaron. Did Henry get in the way?"

"God, no! How could you think something like that?"

Reggie tried to push past her father, but he caught her by the arm.

"Look me in the eye and tell me it was an accident."

Reggie felt her heart pounding inside her ribcage, but she steadied her gaze with her father's.

"It was an accident."

They were both still, staring at each other; Reggie could see Dad's eyes searching her own, trying to read them.

The doorbell rang, and Dad blinked. He let go of Reggie and stepped back. His angry gaze softened into one of sadness.

"I only want the truth from you, Reggie. I can only help if I know what's going on. And I want to help. It's just the three of us now — we have to be there for each other."

The bell chimed again, and Dad left the office. Reggie heard the front door open and Dad's surprised voice.

"Mr. Bloch? It's kind of late — can I help you with something?"

Reggie shot to her feet and strode into the hall. She frowned at Eben, who stood in the doorway, leaning heavily on his cane.

"Yes." Eben took a small step inside. "I know it's late. My apologies for this unexpected visit. But I need to speak with Regina. The matter is urgent."

"I have nothing to say to you."

"Reggie." Dad's voice had an edge.

"May I —" Eben took another small step forward.

"Yes, yes. Come in."

Reggie crossed her arms but said nothing as Eben came inside. He offered her a tired smile, but it did little to disguise the man's palpable agitation.

"Please, Regina. This is about our friend."

Aaron. Reggie's skin burned like coal. How could she have forgotten him, no matter what she'd been through since his arrest that morning?

"Aaron."

"Yes," Eben said softly. "He needs our help."

Reggie looked at her father.

"Five minutes," he said, then walked back into his office.

Eben shuffled inside, and under the full light of the room, Reggie noticed that he appeared much older and frailer than the last time she'd seen him. His skin was pale and blotchy, his eyes sunken and gray. He looked utterly exhausted. He stooped, leaning more on his cane for support than Reggie had remembered.

"I would stand, but I am very tired these days." He crossed to the recliner and took a seat.

"Unless you tell me you can get Aaron out of jail, we've got very little to talk about." Reggie paced behind the living room sofa, arms folded. "And you don't look like you're in shape to pull off a prison break."

"I deserve your rage, Regina. I know that. But hating me isn't going to solve any immediate problems."

Reggie stopped pacing. "I don't hate you, Eben. Come on." She moved to the couch and sat down.

"I want you to tell me what happened today," Eben said.

Reggie rubbed her forehead, the anxiety of the morning coming back to her.

"The police were at school. They came and took Aaron away in front of everyone. For questioning. There were rumors that . . ." Reggie swallowed. "That they found Quinn's car."

"That part I've heard already. I want to know if anything *else* happened today." Eben spoke quietly but intensely. Reggie stared at him for a moment.

"How did you know?"

"Tell me."

Reggie recounted her vision in first period, and Henry's meltdown at school. When she was finished, Eben tented his fingers and was quiet, lost in thought.

"What are we going to do about Aaron?" Reggie asked finally. "That detective was scary serious."

"She's scary, all right," Eben said curtly. "Or rather, *it's* scary."

"*It?*" Horror flooded Reggie. "You mean that woman, she's a . . . she's a *Vour?*"

Eben nodded.

"Many police forces are filled with them. Vours like to infiltrate places of authority, remember? It makes it easier for them to achieve their goals. And tougher for someone like me to get to," he added ruefully.

The fear rocked inside Reggie. "What is their goal? What do they want? I thought it was over."

"I had hoped it was over for you," Eben conceded.

Reggie jumped up. "We have to get Aaron out of there before she hurts him. Or kills him."

"I doubt it will kill him — that would draw unnecessary attention. But it will try to break him."

Reggie held her hand out to Eben.

"Come on, let's go."

"No, Regina, I don't want you anywhere near that station."

"But —"

Eben coughed, and the painful rasp sounded all too familiar to Reggie. For a moment it seemed as if Eben might break into one of his uncontrollable hacking spasms that had started last winter, the kind that ended with blood spilling out onto a white handkerchief.

"Eben, you're in no state to do this on your own."

"I will get Aaron out of there, and I will protect you and your family. But Regina, I need you to promise that you're not going to go looking for trouble with the Vours."

"Eben, I —"

"Promise me. No more hero stuff."

Reggie felt the rage and panic rising inside her; at this point she couldn't tell one from the other.

"I was never trying to be a hero — but you and your . . . secrets! They've led to nothing but suffering and pain! Why won't you tell me what you know? Maybe this could have been prevented if we'd all worked together. Your secrecy hasn't protected anyone but yourself!"

Reggie felt her face flush, and she knew she was yelling loud enough for the whole house to hear, but she didn't care.

"Regina, I know it might seem that way, but you must trust my judgment —"

"And why can't you trust me?" Reggie leaned over Eben. "Tell me what you know. *Tell me!*"

"*Reggie!*" Dad stood in the doorway, shocked. "Stop this. Get away from the man."

He crossed the room in three strides and pulled his daughter away from Eben. Then he helped the elderly man to his feet.

"I think maybe it's time you went home, Mr. Bloch."

"Indeed it is." Eben looked from Thom to Reggie, who was still breathing heavily. He lifted his hand, as if he wanted to embrace her, then thought better of it and lowered it again. "Aaron will be okay, Regina. I'll see to it. And I can see myself out."

With that, he limped to the front door and out into the dark night.

"What was that about?" Dad asked darkly as he locked the door behind Eben.

"Aaron got into some trouble today," Reggie replied, equally coolly. "We just disagree on how to help him."

She started up the stairs, expecting Dad's command to return so they could finish their talk, but none came. At the top of the landing she looked back to see her father sitting on the sofa, his head in his hands.

Reggie turned on the tap in the shower and waited for the water to warm. She had stood here just this morning feeling normal again, and now the day had left her dirty and afraid. She wished she could wash it all away, but the soap just wasn't strong enough.

After her shower she put on her pajamas and brushed her teeth, going through the motions of nighttime rituals as anxiety for the future spread throughout her limbs. Before getting into bed she checked her e-mail; just one was waiting for her, from eb@somethingwicked.com. Reluctantly she clicked it open.

Regina, do put your faith in me. Rest tonight. When I bring Aaron out, that wretched thing will have made its mark on him. He will need you more than ever when this is done.　　—E

Sleep came upon her like an oil spill — greasy and black, flooding and poisoning her dreams with sadness and pain. Nothing gelled into images; the blackness, the fear, the suspicion, and the malice coursed through her subconscious layers like heated blobs of wax.

"Wake up, sleepyhead."

The voice was a whisper. It traveled like a cold breeze and blew through twists and turns in the strange labyrinth of her mind. She heard herself moaning in the dark.

"Aww. That's my girl. Wakey, wakey."

Reggie had experienced such phenomena before, but not since she was a little girl.

"Reggie . . ."

The voice called again, and this time she was sure it had woken her. But she couldn't move, couldn't feel her body in space. She felt only the leaden weight of the darkness. She wafted uneasily in a state between wake and slumber.

The thing calling to her was treading alongside her.

"Reggie . . ."

The voice was now next to her, becoming clearer and more familiar as the darkness receded. Human.

"Reggie . . ."

Closer now.

"Come on now . . ."

On top of her.

Pavor nocturnes.

Night terrors.

"Time to wake up."

She pushed her mind to the surface, willing it to wake. She sprang up in bed.

A lone figure in silhouette sat on the edge of her bed. A pinprick of light, as from a small flashlight, lit a piece of paper the person was reading. Reggie could not make out a single feature on the intruder's face, but she recognized the suppressed laughter.

"Rise and shine."

Reggie panicked and tried to squirm away. The figure in the dark giggled and then clamped its hand down on her knee from atop the thin cotton sheet.

"Quiet, sweet thing. Make a sound and I will slit your throat. No, I'll slit your father's throat first. Then your little shit of a brother will have his. I'll let you watch."

This had to be another nightmarish vision. He couldn't have survived. He couldn't be alive.

"Surprised to see me? Thought I was dead? I'm okay, honest."

He scooted up the bed a few inches.

The beam of the pocket flashlight swung upward and lit the intruder's face.

"Boo."

Reggie cried out and he leaped at her, putting his hand over her mouth and pressing her head down into the pillow. He kept the flashlight under his chin and stared at her with wild, bitter eyes.

"What? Not pretty enough for you anymore?"

The right half of Quinn Waters' face looked normal — the long eyelashes, the dark curls framing a sculpted cheek and jaw, though the latter were paler than Reggie remembered, so white they looked carved from marble. But the left half . . . Despite her terror, Reggie stared at it with fascination. Veins like black scars crisscrossed over his cheek and jaw, and his lips were a wan blue. His eyes, though, were as bright as ever, chilling and lethal.

"Yeah. I know. Get some cover-up, Quinn." He smiled and revealed a set of perfectly white teeth. "Still got the pearly whites though, right? How about you? Life hectic these days?" He moved his hand up and down, forcing her head to nod. "Oh, that's right. Finals week. You must be crazy swamped about now." He leaned in close to her, his breath cold on her face. "If I let you up, no screaming. I *really* don't want us to be interrupted."

He took his hand from her mouth.

"Miss me? What am I saying, of course you missed me." Quinn shook the piece of paper, and Reggie realized it was the scrap she had written her nightmare on the night before. That's what he had been reading. "I don't know if it's touching or pathetic that you're still dreaming about me. Wait, no, I do. It's pathetic." His tone was eerily gleeful.

Reggie sat up, scurrying to the top of the bed. She pulled the sheets up to her neck and drew her knees to her chest. Quinn shook his head and yanked the sheets from her, exposing her legs and feet. She frantically stretched her nightshirt down over her knees, as far down her bare legs as it would go.

"At least you get what's coming to you in your subconscious," Quinn went on. He reached over to her end table and flicked on the lamp. In the light, the whiteness of his skin looked almost translucent.

Reggie trembled as she spoke. "How —"

"How am I still alive?" Quinn shook his head and smirked. "I can tell you one thing, it is no thanks to you, the old man, or your nerd of a boyfriend. Damn, I want to meat-grind that prick."

"Are you going to kill me?"

"Nah. As much as the thought delights me, I didn't come here for that. I have business."

"Business?"

"Yes. See, I can't exactly fit in anymore. You and your associates ruined all that. I was one of the favorites, you know. More human than human. But now . . ."

Quinn pushed a vein on his cheek and a wisp of black smoke seeped out.

"Now I'm just a screwup. And my lot doesn't take kindly to screwups. I've been cast out."

Reggie stayed silent. The Vour inside Quinn had spewed so many lies in the past. It had lived inside the shell of another boy for who knew how many years, and everything it said or did or *was* had been sculpted from lies.

"What can I say, doll? The hunter has become the hunted."

"The other Vours want to destroy you?"

"Hurt, maim, torture. And then, when they're done having their fun, yes. Destroy. For good."

"Sounds fine to me," Reggie said.

Quinn patted her bare foot, and her skin crawled at his touch. She remembered the power it possessed, the freakish ability it had to conjure terrible and paralyzing fears when in contact with a victim. She kicked his hand away.

"What do you want?"

"Simple. Revenge."

"On me?"

Quinn cupped her cheek with his hand.

"Eventually, maybe. But no, not now. My beef is with my brethren, and I need your help."

Reggie shook him off.

"Never."

"I didn't ask for your opinion." He slithered up the side of the bed like a snake, his icy eyes opened wide. "I don't care what you want, or what you think."

He touched her foot again, and Reggie could not move.

"You will give me exactly what I need, Reggie. And when you do, maybe I'll spare your family. Maybe I'll spare your sanity."

He tickled his fingers up her calf like a spider's legs.

"Maybe not."

Reggie squirmed and slapped his hand away. She wanted to scream, she wanted to hurt him before he could hurt anyone else, but her muscles could only tremble beneath her skin. The fear felt like a straitjacket.

Quinn stood up and stretched.

"I can't believe you don't see the beauty of this partnership. Bringing down the Vours is as good for you as it is for me."

"You're an evil bastard."

"I know." Quinn walked to the bedroom door. "But we have a common enemy now. Sweet dreams, princess. I'll be in touch."

6

Reggie sat huddled at the head of her bed. She could barely stretch out on her mattress, much less sleep. She turned on all the lights.

Quinn was alive. And he had been in her bedroom. Reggie tried to shake the terror away.

She'd read through two study guides, a magazine, and four comic books by the time the sun rose, and then she decided to clean her room. Finally, at 8:30, she thought it was late enough to call the Coles'.

Their answering machine picked up after a few rings, but as Reggie was leaving a message she heard a click, and Aaron's mother's voice came over the line.

"Oh, Reggie, is that you? I'm sorry, we've been screening our calls. There's been some press."

"Is Aaron okay? Is he home?"

"He's home, yes." Dr. Cole's voice was strained. "We got him out early this morning."

"Is it . . . would it be all right if I came over?"

Reggie could hear the woman's hesitation.

"Please," Reggie begged. "Just for a bit. I'd like to see him, see if there's anything I can do."

"And I'm sure he'd like to see you," Dr. Cole replied. "I guess that would be fine."

As Reggie was pulling on her jeans the memory of Quinn's fingers creeping up her leg turned her stomach. She attempted, unsuccessfully, to block it out. So instead, she spent most of the fifteen-minute walk over to Aaron's house trying to figure out how to tell him about Quinn. Or if she should even tell him at all.

But all thoughts of Quinn vanished when Reggie rounded the corner onto Aaron's block. Dr. Cole had vastly understated when she'd said there'd been "some press."

Parked cars and TV news vans lined the street in front of the Coles' house. Police held back the crowd milling on the edge of the lawn, and a few cameramen had set up across the street. Local media had found out about a possible new lead in the Quinn Waters case. Reggie imagined a mob of townspeople gathering like the angry villagers from *Frankenstein*, with Aaron as their monster. The stores downtown were probably having a rush for pitchforks and torches at that very moment.

She cut through a few neighboring backyards and made her way to the Coles' back door. Aaron's father answered, his face taut with concern, but he smiled when he saw it was Reggie.

"Hello, Reggie. I was worried you were one of the reporters. Come on in."

"Oh, Reggie!" Dr. Cole pulled Reggie into a bear hug when she saw her. Her eyes were red from crying.

Reggie had often found solace with the Coles, in no small part to Aaron's parents, who treated her like their own daughter. Dr. Cole was a locally well-known therapist who had a weekly radio show on a community channel, and Mr. Cole was an engineer. They were kind and intelligent, and Reggie relished the normalcy of their household, where voices were never raised, meals were home-cooked and on time, and both parents were around to kiss their son goodnight.

She looked around her. The house was spotless as ever, but all the drapes were drawn, and jazz played from the sound system to drown out the activity outside.

"How is he?"

"He's got bruises all down his arms. The Wennemack Police are going to have one hell of a lawsuit on their hands when I'm done with them." Dr. Cole sighed. "He's been in his bedroom since we got back. He won't talk, he won't eat — and you know Aaron always has a healthy appetite. He's exhausted but can't sleep."

"When did you guys get home?" Reggie asked.

"Sometime around two," Mr. Cole said. "I thought they were going to keep us there all night, but then that Mr. Bloch showed up."

"I don't know what that man did," said Dr. Cole, "but ten minutes after he arrived we were signing Aaron out and packing him into the car."

"With a warning not to leave town, of course," Mr. Cole added.

Reggie wondered just what cards Eben held, that he'd been

able to make good on his promise to get Aaron released so quickly.

"Well, I think I'll go up then," she said.

Dr. Cole put a hand on Reggie's shoulder. "Honey, I just want you to be prepared when you see him. He's in a post-traumatic state. Community Mental Health wanted to place him in a hospital. It's a good thing I know a few people on the board — and Dr. Unger, of course." She sucked in her lips and took a breath. "Aaron will be fine, but right now he's a little fragile."

"Don't worry. I just want to see how he's doing," Reggie said, thinking that Aaron's mom had no idea how tough her son actually was. "Thanks."

She made her way to Aaron's room. The door was shut, but she could hear both the radio and the television blaring inside. She knocked loudly and called out, but there was no answer.

Puzzled, Reggie gently pushed the door open and peered inside. Every light in the room was on, along with all three computer monitors, the TV, and the stereo. The noise was deafening. Aaron's bedroom had never been what one would call "tidy," but these days it was a disaster. Energy drink cans littered the floor, and a glacier of printouts leaned against the computer desk. The ripped and tattered remnants of overnight shipping envelopes were scattered everywhere. Reggie assumed they were from the books piled all around. Every title had something to do with ghosts, psychics, secret societies, psychology, or demonic possession. The place had once looked like the bedroom of a teenage horror buff and computer geek. Now it seemed more like the den of an occult-obsessed lunatic.

Aaron slouched in an office chair, wrapped in a blanket. Reggie tried not to stare. His face was drawn and puffy, his eyes sunken and haunted. Though the blanket covered the bruises on his arms, Reggie could see his ripped fingernails scabbed with blood, as if he had been clawing at brick walls. He hugged himself, rocking back and forth in his seat.

Reggie went forward and kneeled in front of him. Only then did he seem to notice her.

"When I found out . . . that *they* had you . . ." She broke off. "I was so worried." She put her arms out to hug him, but he shied away from her touch. He shook his head.

"Sorry." His voice was harsh and clipped.

"What did they do to you?" she asked.

"What they do. What they always do." Aaron cocked his head. Reggie could almost see the effort he made to focus. Then he shut his eyes tightly and twitched. "I can't see, Reggie," he said desperately, starting to rock again. "I can't see out of my head."

Dread creased Reggie's forehead. She had seen Aaron scared before, plenty of times, but never shattered like this. She'd always thought his was a mind of unbreakable logic, but the Vours had broken it. There was no way she could tell him about Quinn, or much of anything else, right now. Anger at the monsters that did this to him seethed inside her.

"Shh, shh," she said, hugging him despite his spasms. "It wasn't real. Whatever they showed you, it was fantasy. Push back, remember? Push back."

Reggie held on to him for a while until Aaron finally seemed calmer. His breathing became more even as his mind fought for control of itself.

"It's all starting again, Reg, isn't it?" he asked.

"I don't know," she replied.

"Are you scared?"

Reggie just nodded.

"Me, too."

⋯⋯

At last Aaron fell into a fitful sleep, and Reggie left the room. She left the stereo blasting, however; he seemed more relaxed when the noise could drown out his thoughts.

Having escaped the media circus outside, Reggie took out her phone to check the time and saw that there were three missed calls — and that she was a half-hour late getting home. Dad had told her at least fifteen times that they'd be leaving at 9:30 to go for the family therapy session, and it was now just after ten. She pressed the voicemail button with dread.

"Reggie, we're leaving here in ten minutes. Where are you?"

"Regina Halloway, you better be walking through that door in *one* minute. Call me back *now*."

"Damn it, Reggie! I asked one thing of you! How could you let Henry down like this? You and I are having a serious talk when I get back."

Reggie's stomach churned with guilt as she pressed the speed dial for her house. The phone rang four times before the answering machine picked up.

"Shit," she muttered, quickening her pace. They'd gone. Her only chance was to catch the next bus that ran out to Thornwood Hospital; she wouldn't be on time for the session, but she figured this was a better-late-than-never scenario.

Reggie ran the last block, and she was damp with sweat by the time she reached her driveway. Dad's truck wasn't there. She pulled out her house keys, and only then noticed the long, skinny white box tied with red ribbon sitting on her front stoop.

Reggie glanced behind her, but no one was around. She looked at the card on the box. "Regina Halloway" it read, in crimson, florid script. With a shaking hand, she picked it up and carried it into the house.

Reggie set the box on the kitchen table and stared at it for a few minutes, half-expecting it to explode. Finally, she undid the ribbon and opened it.

She screamed and pushed the box away. It teetered on the edge of the table and fell, scattering the dainty pink and white flowers that were inside it across the floor. The flowers were covered in a sticky red liquid.

Bleeding Hearts.

Reggie stared down in horror at the monstrous bouquet. The red substance pooled in the grout between the floor tiles. Was it really blood? She didn't want to know.

She fetched a roll of paper towels and cleanser and started mopping up the mess, trying to control her gag reflex. Covering her hand in paper towels, she gingerly lifted the spattered flowers by the stems and carried them to the garbage can; as she did so, a sticky piece of paper fluttered to the ground. Reggie bent down and picked it up.

It was a movie ticket from the Charleston Theater, a place that showed old movies for cheap.

"*The Way We Were*, 11:30 AM, Saturday, June 13," it read. About an hour from now. Written on the back in the same red script that was on the bouquet's card was the note, "Be there, or I'll break your heart."

Reggie felt sick. Flowers and a movie. There was a time when she would have given anything to attract such attention from Quinn Waters. And he knew it.

She gazed at the ticket as she weighed her options. "Rock" and "hard place" came to mind.

If she ignored Quinn's summons she still might be able to make at least part of the therapy session. It would make Dad happy, or at least less mad, and, more importantly, Henry needed her right now. But Quinn had threatened her family, and she knew to take him seriously. If she didn't show, who knew what he might do?

Reggie spoke quietly to herself as she continued to wipe up the gunk on the floor.

"I need to take him out of the equation," she murmured. "It's the only way to protect my family. And there are only two ways I know of to do that. Destroy the Vour and save the real Quinn, or . . ."

Her voice trailed off as her mind finished the sentence.

Kill him.

"Don't be stupid — you can't kill him," she told herself. "There's a real human being locked away in there somewhere."

But another part of her brain, one that sounded a lot like Eben, answered back.

"But you've seen what can happen to a human after coming back from the fearscape. Look at Henry. Look at what he almost did yesterday. Will he ever really recover? Will he ever live a normal life?"

The unanswerable questions poured forth.

What if the Vour wasn't really destroyed?

What if it still existed inside him somewhere?

What if, next time, he took a life?

Even if the monster was dead, what if this was where serial killers came from? Murderers, rapists, all the psychos Aaron read about and studied — what if there were others brought back from the fearscape like Henry, who could never forget the horrors they'd witnessed there? Who coped with the pain of re-membering by making others suffer?

What if rescuing a soul from the fearscape was just dooming it to a different kind of hell in the real world? And dooming other innocent victims to those psychotic crimes?

Reggie's heart reeled, and she could feel the tears welling.

But he's my brother, she thought. *I had to save him.*

But that was just it. Henry was her brother. Quinn was not.

Maybe she had never even known the real Quinn. Maybe he'd been Vourized for so long he couldn't be brought back. And even if he could, what if he was still a monster, having lived in hell for so long?

There were too many maybes, too many what-ifs.

Reggie forced herself to look at facts, and stripping away all uncertainties, there were two:

1. If she didn't help him, Quinn would hurt those she loved most.

2. There was no way she was ever going to help that son of a bitch.

That left one thing for her to do.

7

Reggie pedaled hard, racing her bike across town. It had taken her another twenty minutes to form a plan and gather all the supplies she needed, and now she feared Quinn would arrive at the theater first. She had to get there before him. Her scheme depended on it.

The Charleston Theater was located in a rundown area of Cutter's Wedge. It was an old theater, with tattered curtains that opened and closed in front of the screen and box balcony seats. Two dollars would buy a ticket to whatever old movie was showing, and a couple hours' respite from the summer heat in a dark, air-conditioned room. But the shady locale kept traffic to the Charleston low, if not nonexistent.

Reggie locked her bike to a bike rack outside the theater and went inside to the lobby. She glanced around. The lobby was empty except for the grizzly old man behind the concession stand. She approached the counter.

"Large Mountain Dew, please."

He nodded and shambled over to the drink fountain, taking his sweet time. Reggie kept glancing from the wall clock, which read twenty after eleven, to the front entrance. With every tick of the second hand she expected Quinn to walk in, and her plan would be blown.

Finally the man handed her the soda and collected her money. Reggie snatched the drink off the counter, but she didn't go into the theater right away. Instead, she headed into the women's restroom.

It was an old-fashioned vanity, with round lightbulbs lining the mirror, but several were burnt out. Reggie locked the door and set the soda by the sink, then opened her satchel.

Inside were a bottle of pills and a carving knife.

Calmly, Reggie uncapped the bottle of her father's sleeping pills and dumped a few of them onto the counter. Then she took up the knife and crushed the pills into a powder, using the flat end of the blade. Finally, she swept the powder off the counter and into the soda, stirring the granules into the drink with the straw.

Reggie told herself that morally, she could accept killing Quinn, a Vour. She had to accept it. But physically carrying out the act was a much different thing. The Vour would be gone, but a human body, the victim of foul play, would be left behind. A murder investigation would follow.

As Reggie saw it, the death had to look like an accident, or suicide. Since she couldn't think of a way to make dying in a movie theater look accidental, she had decided on the latter. Quinn, like all Vours, had a wicked sweet tooth, and she was counting on the sugary Mountain Dew tempting him. She had thought about just relying on the sleeping pills to kill him, but she didn't know how many pills that would take, and she couldn't risk stealing too many from her father's supply. Even he would notice an empty bottle.

Reggie went over the plan in her head again.

She'd give him just enough to incapacitate him, so that she could slit his wrists and let him bleed out. She'd wipe the knife, then wrap his hand around it so only his fingerprints were on it, and leave it with him. Then she'd take the Mountain Dew and go home. When they processed the body, tox results would show Quinn had drugs in his system, but not enough, Reggie hoped, to rule out the possibility he had taken them himself in an effort to dull the pain of the knife.

It was a desperate plan filled with holes, she knew. More than anything she wished Aaron were there, to help her with the details, to point out the flaws and how to fix them. But Aaron was in no shape to plot a murder, nor did Reggie want to endanger him in that way. He could not be party to this, in case things went wrong. Plus, once the body was found, Aaron would be cleared. With the press swarming his house, he had a solid alibi.

She unlatched the bathroom door. What would it feel like to stab someone, she thought. To leave them to die? Could she really go through with it?

At 11:29, it was too late for second thoughts. Reggie steeled herself and pushed open the theater door. Her eyes adjusted to the dark, and she saw that it was empty. With equal parts relief and trepidation, she perched on a seat in the back row as the movie projector sprang to life. Animated popcorn started dancing across the screen in front of her, but Reggie paid it no attention. Focus on the plan, she told herself. Focus.

The minutes passed; the advertisements and trailers ended, the feature began, and still no Quinn. Where the hell was he?

Ten minutes. Twenty. Twenty-five. Reggie's anxiety grew — was this a trap? Had she really been so dumb as to come out here by herself?

She was about to get up when the theater door opened a crack, and a beam of light from the lobby outside shone down the aisle. Reggie pulled her satchel onto her lap and slipped her hand inside it, wrapping her fist around the hilt of the knife. A figure in a hoodie leaned heavily on the door, pushing it all the way open, then limped through.

Quinn saw her immediately and collapsed in the chair next to hers, slipping back his hood. Old rags, brown and crusty with dried blood, covered his right hand, and there was a huge gash under his left eye, in addition to the skin markings she'd already seen. Reggie stared at him in horror, and Quinn laughed bitterly.

"That bad, huh? You look even more grossed out than you did last night." His voice was raspy and came in starts, like even speaking was painful.

"What happened?" Reggie asked, curious despite herself.

"My old buddies found my hiding spot, and they decided to stop by for a visit." Quinn coughed and clutched his chest, then saw the large soda. "Please tell me that's not diet." He snatched it up, put the straw to his blue lips, and sucked down half the drink in one gulp. "Ahh. That's better."

Reggie eyed him as he wiped his mouth. She kept her hand on the knife, still hidden in her satchel.

"So Vours did this? Why didn't they kill you?"

"Who says they didn't try?" Quinn held the cold drink up to his eye. "First they played punching bag with me for a while, then Keech brought out the big guns. Or, rather, the big hatchet. Took off two of my fingers before I managed to escape." He pointed to the bloodied bandage and smiled wryly. "Guess now my chances at pro ball are really shot."

"Keech?" Reggie repeated. Quinn grinned, and even in the darkened theater his eyes looked keen like a wolf's.

"Yep. Keech. It's getting more dangerous for me. And for you. I found out his orders are to take care of us both."

"So this is you warning me? Next time just text me or something."

Quinn's smile disappeared.

"I guess self-preservation brings out the dramatic in me. The only way I can survive is to destroy the Vours, and the only way to do that is with your . . . skills . . ." His voice trailed off, and he blinked.

"Why now?" Reggie pressed. She wanted to get as much information out of him as she could before the meds kicked in fully. "The Vours laid low for months. Why come after me now?"

"That's right. Six months." Quinn took another sip of soda. "And what happens six months after Sorry Night?"

Reggie didn't understand at first, but then she recalled Machen's lecture in English class. *Appropriate that exams are just a week before midsummer . . .* She shook her head.

"The solstice. The Vours have power on the summer solstice, too?"

"Usually, no. But this year is different."

"Why?"

"This year they have you." Quinn leveled his eyes with Reggie's. "You changed things, Reggie. You changed the balance. When you stepped foot in that fearscape, all the rules broke."

Reggie's mind flashed back to the night when she'd gone by herself to the old Canfield house, attacked a Vour, and literally swallowed fear. She had ingested a solid form of the demon, made it a part of herself, and this had given her the ability to enter other people's fearscapes. It's how she had saved her brother.

"What rules?"

"Sorry Night's a rule," said Quinn. His voice was starting to sound dreamy. "We can only enter a human's body on Sorry Night. One night a year. It's a hell of a traffic jam getting out of our world and into this one."

Reggie was beginning to see.

"But if it could be any day, any time of year that the Vours could inhabit humans . . . ," she wondered.

Quinn nodded lazily and tapped his finger to his nose.

"Ding ding ding. That's right. Since you broke the rules with Henry, I guess they're looking to try and break a few, too."

"How do I stop it?"

Quinn sighed, and his eyelids drooped. "That's why Keech is after you. So you can't stop it."

"But what is their plan? How are they going to do it?" Reggie shook Quinn by the arm, rousing him. His skin was cool to the touch and thin like paper.

"I don't know what's wrong with me," he said, yawning. "I feel . . ." He glanced at the Mountain Dew, then at Reggie, and another smile stretched across his lips. ". . . drugged. Nice one, Halloway. I should have seen it coming, but I didn't think you had it in you."

Reggie pulled the knife out of the satchel and held it to Quinn's throat.

"Tell me what the Vours' plan is."

Quinn lay back in his seat.

"You know what? Just do it. It will be a relief. No more running, no more hiding. And I'm glad it's you, and not them. You've earned it."

Reggie hesitated, hovering above him, the knife between them. Quinn stared dreamily at her. Even with the bruises, his eyes were still as beautiful as the first time she'd seen them.

"I know it's not easy for you," Quinn continued, his words slurring together now. "It's not easy to kill. But in war, you have to eliminate your enemy. No moral qualms. We're generals, Reggie. We're above that . . ."

His voice trailed off, his head lolled to the side, and his hand slipped off the armrest. The bandage snagged and fell off, and in the flickering light from the movie screen, Reggie saw the stumps of his ring and pinky fingers, chopped right below the knuckles. The wound had opened again and blood burbled up. She shuddered at the grotesqueness of it. Quinn was a monster, but he was still vulnerable, like a human. There was a human boy locked away inside somewhere.

He was weak now; her plan had worked. She could slice him open and leave him to die.

She dropped the knife and it clattered to the floor.

"I don't want to be above it," she said. "That's the difference between you and me."

She stood up, but just at that moment the movie projector clicked off, leaving the theater in silence and dark. The red light of the exit signs glowed eerily.

"Regina Halloway!" A leering voice echoed through the theater. "I'm sorry, did I interrupt your *date*?"

A chill speared through Reggie. She recognized the voice of Keech Kassner. They were here, now.

She slung her satchel over her head and felt on the ground for the knife. The tips of her fingers closed around the cold steel, and with her other hand she felt blindly forward, crawling over Quinn to the end of the row of seats. She yanked on the theater door, but it was locked.

"Not that way," said Keech, and Reggie spun around, holding out the knife with a trembling hand. She couldn't see a thing, and she couldn't pinpoint where the voice was coming from. It was all around her.

"You know you won't get out of here alive," the voice continued, tauntingly. "You're both going to die. A shame, too. You're going to miss all the fireworks."

"What fireworks?" Reggie called into the dark, her voice trembling.

"Armageddon, June twenty-first. I'd tell you to mark your calendar, but you're going to be out of town. Or six feet under it, to be more precise. Too bad you didn't listen to Quinn's warnings."

Reggie stumbled back down the back row of seats where Quinn was passed out. She didn't like it, but she had to admit he might be her only hope of figuring out the Vours' plans. If they could even get out of here. She shook him by the shoulders.

"Quinn, wake up," she whispered.

"Wha? Huh?" he moaned, shifting in his seat.

Reggie dumped the remaining Mountain Dew on him and slapped him hard across the face. Blood from his wounds wet her fingers.

"Wake up!" she urged.

Quinn sat up groggily. "It's still dark out, Mom. Not time for school . . ."

Reggie heaved him up out of the chair, slinging his arm around her shoulder to support him.

"It's Reggie. We are still in the theater and Keech is here!" she hissed.

Keech's laughter boomed through the blackness.

"Wait, did Quinn fall asleep on you? *Awwkward.*"

Quinn seemed to come to a little. "Keech? He'll kill us!"

"No shit! Come on, I need you to walk." Reggie half pulled, half dragged him into the aisle, his feet slow to respond. Together they stumbled toward the front of the theater where another red sign showed the emergency exit. Reggie held her hands out in front of her, praying they wouldn't run straight into Keech. They reached the door, but it was locked, too.

"Not that way, either," said Keech.

Reggie looked around, frantic. They were trapped. Quinn slumped against her.

"Reggie, did you like the flowers I sent you?" he asked sleepily.

"Not helping!" Reggie took a step and bumped into the stage.

She propped Quinn against it. "We have to find another way out of here."

She heard a noise, and a match flared at the back of the theater. Behind its glow she could see Keech's hulking outline, stalking slowly toward her.

"Nowhere to run," he said.

She hauled Quinn across to the other aisle, but then another match blazed, and a second figure, identical to Keech in size and shape, came forward. Keech's twin brother, Mitch.

Reggie backed away. Keech's match went out, and he lit another. Reggie could see his snarl, but Mitch looked stoic. Reggie shuddered at their determination.

And then, in the dim light of the matches, Reggie saw it. A ladder built into the theater wall leading up to the box seats. It was just a few feet away from her. With Quinn in tow, Reggie sidled toward the ladder, not wanting to give away her plan to the Kassners. They still approached slowly, savoring their victory, their kill.

"Quinn," she said quietly through her teeth. "Are you still with me?"

Quinn lifted his head off her shoulder and sighed.

"Yep. I'm here. Hey, I like your hair cut like that."

Reggie rolled her eyes and brandished the knife.

"I need you to *focus*," she said, nicking him in the arm with the knifepoint. This finally seemed to jolt Quinn awake.

"Hey!"

Reggie thrust him against the wall.

"Climb!" she ordered.

Immediately, Keech realized what she was up to, and he and Mitch rushed at her. Reggie waved the knife at them.

"Back off!"

Keech laughed. It sounded like a growl.

"You can't take us both on, Halloway. And you just sacrificed yourself for your archnemesis. You are so pathetically human."

Quinn had reached the top of the ladder, ignoring the pain in his hand, and disappeared into the box seat. Reggie continued to swing the knife at a merry Keech and a solemn Mitch, but her mind was blank with terror. There was no way to climb without letting go of her only weapon. Fight or flee, they'd kill her.

A roar and a flash of light came from above. All three of them looked up to see the musty velvet curtain hanging next to the box seat go up in flames. The dry fabric crackled and smoked, then plummeted toward them, a giant fireball. Keech and Mitch dove out of the way, but Reggie leaped onto the ladder and scrambled up as quickly as she could, always expecting a hand to clamp down on her ankle and yank her off. Her arms shook violently with fear, and the black smoke billowing around her choked and blinded her. Suddenly she felt a hand on her shoulder. It heaved her up and over the side of the box. She collapsed on the ground, coughing, as Quinn put his lighter back in his pocket. They stared at each other for a moment, then Quinn pulled her up, and they fled the box to the open air of the theater lobby.

"Do you believe me now?" Quinn grunted as they dashed out the theater's back entrance into the alley. He yanked the hoodie up over his head and pulled it tight.

Reggie didn't answer — she was trying to steady her breath after taking in all the smoke from the burning curtain. Her left forearm throbbed with pain, and she looked down to see a splotch of badly blistered skin. In her rush to escape, the curtain had burned her and she hadn't even felt it.

"I have . . . to get . . . home," she rasped.

"Yeah, we should split up anyway," Quinn said. His speech was slow and slightly slurred, remnants of the sleeping meds. He shook his head, trying to wake fully. "I doubt he'll come after you at your house. He doesn't want to be tied to any crimes. Stay there and in public places."

Reggie's hands shook, and she fumbled with her bike lock. Quinn took the key from her impatiently and snapped open the lock, then dragged the bike off the rack with his good hand.

"And what are you going to do?" Reggie forced herself to control her voice, and yanked the handlebars away from Quinn. She was embarrassed to appear so anxious in front of him.

"Find out what I can. Now you know the stakes, maybe you won't come after me with sleeping pills and a knife."

"Don't bet on it." As she got on her bike, Quinn was already slouching to the end of the alley.

"I'll contact you!" he shouted over his shoulder at her.

"Yeah, and what am I supposed to do in the meantime, wait around for the end of the world?" Reggie yelled after him, but Quinn was already gone.

8

Reggie was relieved to pedal into an empty driveway when she got home: her father and Henry were still out. She showered first, washing the soot and grime off her skin and out of her hair, and threw her dirty clothes in the hamper. She rubbed antiseptic on her burn; there were no bandages in the house large enough to cover the wound, so she put on a thick plastic bangle that mostly hid it. She didn't want her father asking any questions about it.

She took out the trash with the bloody bleeding hearts in it and replaced the bag. Then she sat down at the kitchen table to wait. When Dad got home, she figured she might as well get the drama over with.

She drummed her fingers on the table. The summer solstice. Armageddon. It was a lot to have to think about when she should be studying for finals.

She heard the truck pull up a half-hour later. When they walked in, Henry gave Reggie a sympathetic look, but Dad walked straight to the sink and got a glass of water. He took a long gulp, then filled the glass again.

"Hen, why don't you go play in your room for a bit?" he said.

Henry nodded and left the kitchen. Dad finished the second water and came back to the table. He sat down heavily and only then allowed his eyes to focus on his daughter.

"Do we need to get you a new watch?" he asked.

Reggie looked at her hands.

"Because I believe I was very clear on the time we were leaving this morning. Am I wrong?"

"No, you were clear."

"Then explain to me why at nine o'clock I go into your room to find an empty bed and then can't get a hold of you on your cell phone. That phone is a privilege, not a right. When I call, you pick up."

"Dad, it was an emergency. Aaron —"

"Aaron? Aaron had an emergency? And you chose . . ." Dad's teeth clenched. "Look, I know you have issues with me, but this time I thought . . . because it was Henry. That you'd be there for him."

"Dad, I wanted to be — I did. It was a mistake, I know. Things have just been so crazy."

"Things will always be crazy, Reg. That's life. But your brother should be a priority." Dad spoke softly but firmly, and Reggie could tell he was trying to keep his temper in check. "When you do things like this, he sees that you have more important things in your life than him."

"I'm trying to protect him! I'm trying to protect all of you!" Reggie looked as surprised as her father at her outburst. She bit her lips and kept her head down, and tried to keep the tears at bay.

"Protect us? Reggie, get control of yourself. Look, I'm not going to punish you," Dad continued. "Lord knows that hasn't worked in the past anyway. I need you to work through this and be the sensible girl I know you are. Dr. Unger said you may be reacting to discipline reserved for a child, so I won't do it. And in return I'm expecting you to act like an adult."

"Is that what Dr. Unger said?" Reggie asked wryly. It was probably true in most teenage girls' cases. Reggie already felt like an adult, and it was the last thing she wanted to be.

Dad took one of Reggie's hands in his and looked pleadingly at her. It was an awkward gesture, because Dad was not prone to physical affection with his daughter, but she couldn't hold his gaze.

"Reggie, my greatest fear is to lose you like I lost your mother. And it scares me to see you checking out on us like she did. Please make an effort, if not for me, then for Henry. I don't know if he can take someone else leaving him."

Dad let go of Reggie's hands, put his palms on the table, and pushed himself up out of his chair. Reggie watched him go out into the hall and heard the door to his office close. A minute later, Henry's head appeared in the doorway.

"I heard what he said." He came into the kitchen and wrapped his arms around Reggie's shoulders.

"Henry, you have to believe that I didn't mean to miss your appointment today."

"I know that." Henry pulled away and Reggie saw concern in his eyes. "Was it the Vours?"

Reggie pursed her lips. She didn't want to worry Henry, but she didn't want to lie to him either. She nodded.

"But I want you to know that everything's going to be okay," she said.

Henry stood quietly for a moment, playing with the hem of his T-shirt. His brow furrowed.

"What is it, Hen?"

Henry squinted his eyes and scrunched his face, like he did when he was trying to figure out the answer to a math problem.

"Something happened last night, Reggie," he said finally. "I woke up in the middle of the night and I felt funny."

"Felt funny how? Like you were sick?"

"No. My skin felt weird, like all the heat was being sucked out. It was kind of prickly. Like something was pulling at me."

Reggie frowned.

"Did it hurt?"

"No. It just felt freaky."

"Are you sure you weren't dreaming?"

"No, I thought maybe there was something on my skin, so I went to the bathroom to try to wash it off. But then, when I was in the hall, it got even stronger. Like a *whoosh*, sucking all the heat right out of me. What, Reggie? What's the matter?"

Reggie's lower jaw had dropped open.

"Nothing. That's just really strange, isn't it? I'll talk to Aaron about it — maybe he'll know what it is. Let me know if you feel this way again, okay?"

"Okay. Hey, want to play War?"

"Yeah I do." Reggie got out of her seat and followed her brother upstairs, but her mind was far from cards.

Quinn had been upstairs last night in her own room, mere feet from where Henry slept. Henry's chills had woken him, and increased when he was in the hall, even closer to Quinn. Could it be that Henry had some kind of physical Vour detector inside him? Maybe his experience in the fearscape had left him hyper-sensitive to the monsters' presence.

It wasn't totally far-fetched. And Reggie appreciated the possibilities of being able to immediately recognize her foes, though she didn't like the idea of putting Henry in their proximity. Still, if such an ability existed, it was sure to help their side — she made a mental note to mention this discovery to Aaron the next time she saw him.

But when Reggie called the Cole house Sunday afternoon, Aaron was still sleeping. Dr. Cole didn't want to wake him, and she told Reggie that Aaron would be missing school the following day for doctors' appointments. Reggie guessed Dr. Cole had set up psych visits for her son to deal with his traumatic experience.

School went by excruciatingly slowly on Monday, and Reggie found it hard to concentrate on exam reviews. The other students steered clear of her, whispering and pointing as she passed them. Being the best friend of the kid police thought had something to do with the Quinn Waters case, and the sister of the kid who'd nearly killed a classmate last Friday, hadn't done anything to boost her popularity. Not to mention her freak-out in class.

Reggie sat by herself under a tree in the quad at lunch. As she munched listlessly on a turkey sandwich, her thoughts turned to Aaron. He hadn't contacted her since she'd seen him at his house, and this worried her. What if the Vours really had cracked his mind? The summer solstice was less than two weeks away, and if the event Quinn had warned her about was real, she needed to find a way to stop it.

"See any good movies this weekend?" a gruff voice called out to her, and in the hot sun Reggie felt her skin prick with chills. Keech and Mitch Kassner stood on the sidewalk in front of her. Keech smirked at her, but Mitch hung back, looking at the pavement. Reggie scrambled to her feet.

"Stay away from me." She felt in her satchel for the pepper spray she always carried with her.

"I may look like a dumb jock, but I'm not stupid enough to go after you in front of all these people. That's where your little brother went wrong, you know. Never attack someone on the playground. Should've waited 'til he had the kid alone."

"Shut up!"

"Why are you talking to that chick, Kassner? You know she hangs out with that kid, Cole." Rodney Perez, a tackle for the football team, walked up to them and stared at Reggie. "How does your sick little friend feel about lethal injection?"

The bell rang, and the wave of students eating outdoors moved toward the school's entrance. Rodney gave Reggie one last glare, then turned and followed the crowd.

"All alone, Halloway," Keech said, grinning at Reggie, then he said under his breath, "better watch your back."

He and Mitch ran to catch up with Rodney, leaving Reggie standing by the tree. She realized there was one thing she could do until she heard from Quinn again: get rid of their most immediate threat. Keech.

Her mind flashed to Eben — he had, after all, worked some kind of miracle to get Aaron out of jail. Should she bring him in on this? She dismissed the thought quickly. He would have only one recourse for dealing with Keech, and after her experience in the theater, Reggie had chosen a different path. She didn't need Eben.

She needed Aaron.

9

Reggie checked her phone in her locker at the end of the day and was relieved to see the text.

> Been cooped up 2 long. Muddy's @
> 4? Bring ur books. Just b/c my brain's
> toast, doesn't mean I'm going 2 let u
> fail bio. A

Her mood lightened. If Aaron was joking he must be feeling better. Not that her impending bio flameout was very funny.

When she walked into Muddy's Coffeehouse twenty minutes later, Aaron was in a back booth with a baseball hat on, textbooks and notes spread out over the table. His skin was pale, but his focus seemed as intense as ever as his eyes flitted across the page in front of him.

"Hey," Reggie said, throwing her satchel in the bench across from his. "How were your 'appointments' today?"

Aaron looked up with a thin smile.

"Heady. It's hard work trying to convince shrinks that you don't need them."

"Are you sure you're up for this?" Reggie asked as she slid into the vinyl-covered seat. "We could do this at my house."

"I need to be *out*, Reggie. I can handle the stares and the talk, but I'm done holding up the walls in my bedroom."

"Good. I'm glad to hear that."

"Besides, this isn't about me. We're here to bump you into the prestigious tier of the three point *eight* GPA."

Reggie instinctively reached for Aaron's hand across the table. "How are you?"

"I'll live. The cops made a formal statement to the press and took the heat off me as a suspect, so the media circus on my front lawn has died down."

"So this was just a scare tactic then? No charges?"

"There was never any hard evidence. Everything was circumstantial and Gale knew it. I think the Vours just wanted to rattle our cages. Wish I knew why."

Reggie let this pass for the time being. She had to tell Aaron about Quinn and Keech, but she wanted to do it in the right way.

"Nightmares or visions or anything?"

Aaron opened his biology text.

"I mean, what do you think, Reg?" he said quietly. "Every time I close my eyes. Sometimes when my eyes are open. But I'll deal."

Reggie smiled at him.

"Need a refill?"

"I haven't yet figured out how to mainline the caffeine into my bloodstream, so, yes."

Reggie went to the counter and ordered two large iced coffees. As she set Aaron's cup down in front of him the bracelet on her right wrist slipped aside, revealing her burn. Aaron grabbed her hand.

"What is this?"

"It's . . ." Reggie swallowed. This had not been the right way she had envisioned.

Aaron squinted at Reggie, all good humor gone from his eyes.

"The last time you showed up with burns like this you'd gone off by yourself to Macie Canfield's place where Quinn almost killed you. What aren't you telling me?" His grip on her hand tightened.

Reggie pulled away and covered the burn with the bracelet again, but Aaron continued to stare at her.

"Saturday," she said in a low voice. "After I left your house. Keech Kassner attacked me. Aaron, he's a Vour."

"Christ, Reggie! You thought you'd wait 'til the second cup of coffee to fill me in on this?"

"I didn't want to freak you out. Not after . . ."

"Tell me everything."

Reggie launched into the story but left Quinn out for the moment. She wanted Aaron to get used to her plans for Keech before she sprang the return of their archnemesis on him.

When she was finished, Aaron shook his head.

"No one could be such a lowlife and *not* be an actual demonic life-form. What about Mitch? Is he one, too?"

"Mitch was there, but I don't think he's a Vour. I think he was just following his brother's orders. God, it must be awful for him."

"Or he gets off on it."

Aaron chewed at his cheek. Reggie knew he was taking it all in, weighing the possibilities and consequences of what had happened.

"What are you thinking?" she asked.

"Well, the June twenty-first thing accounts for why all hell broke loose last Friday," he said. "If those psychopaths have something big planned for that date, it's possible they would try to neutralize anyone who poses a threat to them. Get me arrested, kill you, drive Henry crazy . . ."

"Just your typical Friday night fun."

"I'll read up on whatever I can find on the solstice. But Reggie, it's less than two weeks away."

"I know that." Reggie took a deep breath. "And that's why we can't have anyone coming after us."

"You mean Keech?"

"Yeah."

Aaron nodded. "We need him gone. I know you don't want to hear this, but this is Eben's expertise. Together we'll figure out a way to take him out."

Reggie felt a spasm in her chest.

"No, not Eben. I don't want to *kill* Keech."

Aaron frowned at Reggie as her intention dawned on him. "No. No way. You're not going into that sociopath's fearscape."

Reggie took a sip of her coffee.

"I've thought about this, Aaron. I've gone over all the options. We need Keech out of our way, and there are two ways to do it. I won't kill him. And that's why we can't tell Eben. There is a boy in there somewhere who's lived in unspeakable terror for God knows how long. And I have an ability now that can *save* him."

Aaron tugged at the cardboard sleeve on his coffee cup, working the paper between his fingers.

"Great power equals great responsibility? Is that the crap you're feeding me?" His voice was harsh, but he kept it low and controlled. "Vours are pure evil. They enjoy the torture, the torment that they inflict. They deserve to die."

"Yes, but there's a human being that deserves to live," Reggie insisted. "I can save him."

"Do you know that for sure? You don't know what's in that fearscape. For that matter, you don't even know how long it's been around. The way you described Henry's fearscape, it sounded like it was still forming, still shaping itself. Easy compared to others you'd face. And even if it wasn't, Henry is your brother. I get it. But you'd risk your life for *Keech Kassner*?"

Reggie forced herself to stay calm. She couldn't blame Aaron's frustration with her.

"The real Keech Kassner is a scared little boy living in hell, not the bully we know. How can I choose to save one and not the other, just because one's related to me? Humanity is what separates us from them. It can be a thin line, and I don't want to be on the wrong side."

The cardboard sleeve was in shreds on the table.

"Reggie, have you ever considered that it might *be* more humane for them to die?"

"Do you hear yourself?"

"When I was in that prison — the things they made me see, made me feel — I wanted it all to be over. I wanted to *die*. A fearscape must be so much worse. Maybe it's not wrong, Reggie. Maybe it's mercy."

"I'm not God. I won't play that role. And neither will you."

Aaron slammed his hands down on the table, and coffee sloshed out of his cup. A woman at the next booth looked over; Reggie rushed to mop up the spilled coffee with a napkin.

"Look, Aaron, there's something else you need to know."

"Oh God, there's more?"

"It's about Henry. I think he's gained an ability from his time in the fearscape."

"What kind of ability?"

"I think he can sense Vours. Or at least feel when one is near."

"How?"

Now was the time, Reggie thought. Tell him about Quinn in your bedroom. How Henry felt his presence there. How it was through Quinn that they just might discover the Vours' solstice plot.

"The other night . . ." Reggie began, but she couldn't finish. Aaron looked at her expectantly, his body tense and his eyes alert. He could barely accept that Keech should be saved — how could he deal with Quinn being alive, and that Reggie was considering teaming up with him? Aaron wouldn't see that even though Quinn was the enemy, he might be their only chance of stopping the Vours. There was too much hurt there, too much anger. He might even try to kill Quinn himself. She couldn't risk it. "The other night Henry told me he'd felt strange at school, right before he started remembering his fearscape. Like something was sucking the heat out of him. I think he was feeling the presence of a Vour."

"Wow. That's weird, Reg. We know they crave heat, but I never would have guessed they literally pulled it out of everything around them. Maybe being inhabited by a Vour left Henry's body super-sensitive to the loss of physical energy?"

"Something like that."

"It could come in handy —"

"No. Henry stays out of this."

Aaron's eyes looked pained.

"Are you absolutely positive you don't want to tell Eben about any of this? What about the solstice plot? Maybe he knows something about it. He could help."

"He'd tell us to stay out of it, and he'd demand to know where we got our information. You know he would. Then he'd kill Keech. No, I don't want to play by his rules."

"Okay, okay. I get it. So what do you want me to do?"

"I need a way to get into Keech's fearscape. Will you help me?"

Aaron sighed.

"Do you even have to ask?"

"Enjoying your little date?" Nina Snow stepped up to their table and hovered over them. She glowered at Aaron. "Like you even have the right to be walking around when Quinn is probably at the bottom of that lake. What did you do to him?"

"Leave him alone. He didn't do anything," Reggie said.

"The cops just wanted to quiz him on Shakespeare, then?"

"They asked him some questions. They've asked a lot of people questions, remember? Even you."

"What, are you his publicist?" Nina's eyes blazed. "Can't he speak for himself?"

"I don't know why the cops pulled me in," Aaron said. "They're following every piece of evidence, but it had nothing to do with me. I had nothing to do with Quinn."

"He paid you to do his homework. You don't think I knew about that? And he was always nice to you! He talked to you when no one else would!" Nina was growing hysterical. "Everyone knows you're a freak, Cole. You read books about serial killers! Did you kill Quinn?"

Nina was shouting, and the entire café was watching.

"What did you do, you freak? *What did you do?*"

Reggie jumped up.

"That's enough! Leave us alone."

"You probably helped him!" Nina screamed, and she picked up Reggie's iced coffee and dumped it on her. Reggie fell back in her seat in shock; the brown liquid ran down her hair onto her cheeks and T-shirt, spread out across the booth, and dripped onto the floor.

Nina sobbed and ran out of the door.

The coffeehouse was quiet for a minute, then a low buzz filled the room as people went back to their conversations, trying to pretend like they hadn't seen what just happened. A barista hurried over with towels to clean up the spilled coffee, and Reggie patted her face and clothes.

Aaron started packing up his stuff. "I changed my mind. Maybe we *should* study at your place."

<hr/>

Exams started on Wednesday, and Reggie tried to stay focused through French and geometry. But Quinn hadn't made contact, and not knowing if she could trust him made thinking about verb conjugations and theorem proofs impossible. When she wasn't studying, she and Aaron were trying to figure out a way to get Keech someplace cold and remote where Reggie could get into his fearscape. This was a lot harder to do than it was in December. There were no frozen lakes, no snowstorms . . .

"The trouble is," Aaron said on their way home from school Wednesday afternoon, "it's not even like we just have to incapacitate him, which would be hard enough. Mitch never leaves his side — we've got to take out *two* Cro-Magnons."

Reggie kicked a stone along the sidewalk.

"Maybe that's how we get at Keech."

"Kidnap his twin and hope he comes looking for him?"

"No. We get Mitch to help us."

"What?" Aaron chuckled. "I think you inhaled too much lead from those Scantron sheets."

"Hear me out. I noticed on Saturday, and then again the other day, the way Mitch acts. He follows Keech and obeys him because he has to. He's just a —"

"Victim? Are you kidding me?"

"He could be an ally in this. He knows the horrors — don't you think he'd want his brother back more than anyone?"

"Risky." Aaron switched his backpack to his other shoulder. "Risky, but possible."

"We're out of time and options. But those two are inseparable, you're right about that. We need to get Mitch alone."

"I think I have an answer to that one," Aaron said as they rounded the corner onto Reggie's driveway. Dad was standing by his truck.

"An answer to what?" he asked.

"Oh, um . . ." Reggie hesitated.

"Just a math problem on our final," Aaron jumped in.

"Right. Your tests started today. How were they?"

"Character building," Reggie replied.

Dad opened the driver's side door.

"I've got to pick up some lumber in Wennemack, but I'll be home before dinner. Any requests?"

Leaving Dad with a short grocery list, they went inside the house, and Aaron shared his plan with Reggie. They both agreed it was as good as anything they'd got, but it meant waiting until the end of the week. It was common school gossip that each Friday afternoon the Kassner twins had to report to their probation officer in the juvenile center temporarily housed down the street from the Cutter's Wedge Police Station. While Keech was meeting with the probe, they'd have a chance to talk to Mitch alone, if they could get him to listen.

Friday rolled around and Reggie took her last final, the dreaded biology. As she was walking to her locker afterward to clean it out, Mr. Machen stopped her outside his classroom.

"Reggie, would you mind coming in here a sec?"

She followed him to his desk, where he sat down and shuffled through some blue books. He pulled out the one Reggie recognized as her own, with her essay written in purple ink.

"Your essay . . . well, let's just say it surprised me."

He handed the booklet to her, and she almost dropped it on the floor. A red D was scrawled across the cover. Reggie didn't know what to say.

"I'm just used to seeing good work from you," Machen went on. "After the . . . episode last Friday, and the incident at the elementary school — I just wanted to make sure you were okay."

"Things have been a little crazy lately," Reggie admitted. Had she really gotten a D on her English paper? She'd never gotten a D on anything before. "I don't suppose there's any way I could redo the exam or something?"

Machen shook his head.

"I'm afraid not. But your work has been excellent up to now, so this will only bring your semester grade down to a B."

"So much for that three point eight," Reggie muttered.

"I'm sorry, Reggie. I just felt like I should talk to you personally about this, rather than you wondering when your report card came out. You are a great student and a bright girl. Now, you're not going to get into any trouble this summer, right?"

I'm about to go get into trouble right now, as a matter of fact, Reggie thought, but she shook her head at her teacher.

"Well then, have a good break, and we'll see you in the fall."

"Thanks, Mr. Machen. Great class."

Reggie went back into the hall and headed to her locker. She was still holding the blue book, and she dumped it in the trash with the rest of the assorted papers, magazines, and food wrappers that had collected in her locker over the past several months. Kids around her were doing the same thing, and the air was riotous with yelling and laughing. Finally, it was summer vacation.

And a week to the solstice.

Aaron came up behind her.

"Freshman year," he said. "We made it. And with only one body possession and one accidental death to our names."

"The key is surviving until sophomore year," Reggie replied. Her phone rang and she checked it; she didn't recognize the number. She pressed the talk button and put the phone to her ear.

"Hello?"

"Meet me. Right now."

Quinn.

Reggie smiled at Aaron and put up a finger.

"I can't right now," she said, trying to sound casual.

"You want to know what's going down next weekend, you need to see what I found. Now."

"Okay, okay, I get it."

"The old train trestle along the river, the one by the bike path. You know where I mean?"

"Yeah, I know."

"Get there." The line clicked. Reggie flipped her phone shut.

"Who was that?" Aaron asked.

"Um, it was my dad," Reggie said. "A family therapy session for Henry. I missed the last one because, well, you know. I have to go."

Aaron looked puzzled and distressed.

"He said . . . he said he'd track me down at school if I didn't go home."

"Reg, we're not going to get another chance at this."

"I know, I know." Reggie tried to think.

"I'll go myself."

"No way, I can't ask you to do that."

"You're not asking, I'm deciding. I'll go talk to Mitch."

"He could hurt you."

"Nah, I'll be fine." Aaron tried to sound braver than he felt. "But do you mind if I borrow your pepper spray?"

10

The outdoor afternoon heat was a shock after the school's frigid air-conditioning, and the humid air stuck to Reggie like wet paper. There was some traffic on the roads, but not much, and it was an easy bike ride west toward Abernathy Flats. She pedaled past Cutter's Lake and turned onto the bike path that ran along the Wampassee River. Ahead she could see the train trestle that crossed over the water. This was her destination.

Reggie hid her bike behind a bush by the side of the path, and crawled along the river's edge until she was underneath the trestle. Sun filtered through the track slats, crisscrossing the ground in light and shadow. These tracks were no longer in use, having been decommissioned some seventy years earlier when the depot was relocated to downtown Cutter's Wedge, and the entire structure had fallen into disrepair. Pieces of rotted wood lay strewn about the ground, and gaps in the track above Reggie's head suggested that crossing it would be dangerous.

Still, Reggie had to admit, it was an excellent place to camp out in secret. No one except the occasional cyclist or runner passed by, and the bridge's foundation formed a makeshift shelter, hidden from sight from both the bike path and the train tracks. And it was clear someone had been here: empty food cans littered the dirt, and a ripped tarp lay off to the side. Rock chunks were arranged in a circle around scorched earth that Reggie guessed was a fire pit. She chewed at her lip: this was a pitiful existence.

Reggie checked her watch. 3:45. Keech's session with his probation officer was from 4–4:30. If she could get this over with quickly, she still might be able to get back in time to help Aaron.

Quinn, however, was nowhere in sight, so Reggie sat down under the trestle to wait. Butterflies flitted around her stomach, just as they used to do when she saw Quinn Waters by his locker or anticipated his arrival in study hall. She didn't like the feeling.

Her brain was split down the middle: half insisted she was an idiot for pursuing this alliance, but the other half conceded that she didn't have a whole lot of other places to turn. She refused to consider that she might actually be worried about Quinn since she hadn't heard from him in a few days.

Her reverie was interrupted by a noise across the water. She squinted, peering over the wide river. The sound was the revving of a motorbike driving on the far bank. Ahead of it a figure half-ran, half-limped desperately forward. A backpack was slung over his shoulder, and he turned back every so often to see the bike gaining. Black marks stood out against his pale skin — it was Quinn, and someone was chasing him.

Neither of them had apparently seen Reggie, and she waited in the shadows, watching. Quinn reached the river and jumped in. His body shuddered violently in the cool water, which came to his chest, and he tried to hold up his mutilated hand, still wrapped in rags. Though the current was not terribly strong, he struggled to wade forward to the middle of the river, and only then did he turn around to face his pursuer.

The biker had pulled up at the river's edge and stared after Quinn. Then he reared his bike back and plowed onto the train tracks, racing up onto the bridge. Clumps of dirt and rot plunked into the river as the bike rushed forward. The biker braked again in the center of the bridge and looked at Quinn below, still hesitating in the water.

Was it Keech? Reggie wondered. Had he come to finish the job he'd been ordered to do?

The cold river was taking a toll on Quinn's already weak body; the skin surrounding his many cuts and gashes was turning black. His indecision was killing him. Even from her hiding place Reggie could see his teeth chattering.

Quinn continued on toward her side of the bank. He moved slowly, and at one point the river dipped so the water came up to his neck. He wobbled and his hand fell into the water. Quinn shrieked with pain and stumbled forward. He'd be far too weak to fight off the biker once he reached the bank.

The biker seemed to be thinking the same thing, and he didn't move until Quinn was within fifteen feet of the shore. Then he gunned his motorbike and charged the rest of the way across the bridge.

Reggie didn't have time to think. She picked up a rock from the fire pit and hurled it at the rotting slats above her. It broke through a plank and wood splinters showered down around her, leaving a hole in the track above just as the bike was passing. The front tire hit the hole and sank through, jarring the bike to a stop. The biker flew off the front and over the side of the train tracks, falling headfirst onto the rocks below and landing just a few feet from Reggie, motionless.

She turned back to see Quinn emerging from the river, shivering but grinning. The overturned motorbike's engine idled on the bridge overhead and then stalled out.

"I — I didn't mean to," Reggie stammered.

"I'm glad you did." Quinn knelt down beside the still biker. Reggie hovered behind him, biting at her nails.

"Is he . . . did I . . . kill him?"

"Not a him." Quinn wrenched the helmet off the biker's head. Detective Gale's blond hair spilled over the rocks. A gasp escaped Reggie's lips.

Blood trickled down Gale's cheek, but her eyes fluttered open and stared up at Quinn. She opened her mouth to speak.

"Shhh," Quinn said, caressing the sides of her head. Then he jerked his hands sideways and snapped her neck.

Reggie heard the *crack* and stumbled backward. She felt the bile in her throat and vomited on the rocky ground.

"Ew. No goodnight kiss for you," Quinn said.

"Why'd you do that?" she demanded, wiping her mouth with her sleeve. "She was . . ."

"A Vour. She was supposed to kill us, and she was going to die anyway. I made it fast and painless. Better than she deserved." He pointed at Gale. "Check it out."

Black smoke oozed from the woman's mouth, nostrils, and open, unseeing eyes, chilling the air. It gathered into a boiling cloud of inky darkness, undulating a few feet over her wrecked body. Reggie stood frozen with horror as one of its plumes formed into a malevolent humanoid face. Waves of hatred and evil pulsed from its gaze, reverberating though Reggie like a passing freight train. The thing made a hissing, droning sound, and then it sailed off over the river and was gone.

"That's how they check out if you get them by surprise," Quinn said. "All kinds of weird shit happens. Usually we can vacate a body before it fails. Not always, though."

Reggie felt her head spin. She sat down hard on the ground, clutching her temples.

"I can't believe I came here."

"Relax," Quinn said, squatting down by the fire pit. "It just looks like a motorcycle accident. No one will suspect a thing."

Reggie's head shot up.

"That's not the point," she said hotly. "You . . . killed her. She was weak—I could have gone into her fearscape. We could have gotten her to a hospital . . . we could have *saved* her."

Quinn shook his head and chuckled ruefully.

"As much as I appreciate your using the 'we' pronoun, you just don't get it. Gale was a powerful Vour. Stronger than me. She would have decimated you. Fight the battles you can win, Halloway."

"I helped kill her."

"If she had made it over here she would have killed us both."

Quinn pulled off his wet shirt and sat down on a large rock

hot from the sun. Reggie couldn't help but stare, and she felt ashamed for it. He was lean from months of living in exile, bruised and lacerated from the recent attempts on his life, but his broad shoulders and chest were still cut like a boxer's and his arms curved with muscle. In the warm light, the black marks surrounding his wounds were beginning to fade under his ghostly pale skin. He gingerly unwrapped the soaked rags from his hand, wincing when they came off fully. He looked like he was wearing a black glove that was missing two fingers.

"Kind of cool, in a Darth Vader way," he said. He grinned at Reggie, but she could see he was in tremendous pain.

"Will it heal?" she asked.

"I guess we'll see. Hey, I think there are some dry clothes up there." He pointed back to the trestle foundation. "Would you mind —?"

Reggie rummaged around the makeshift camp until she found a couple of T-shirts, then returned to Quinn. He started tearing one in strips using his teeth, then rewrapped his hand.

"Why was she after you?" Reggie asked as he worked.

"I found something," he said. "I was scouting out information at an old compound we used to use as a headquarters. It was mostly cleaned out, but not completely. They'd turned the place into storage for old paperwork. I just had to bide my time getting in and out of there."

Quinn held out his hand to Reggie, and she tied the ends of two strips together, securing the bandage. As she pulled the knot tight, he grabbed her wrist with his good hand. Reggie cried out.

"Hey! Let go of me!"

But Quinn had taken Reggie's hands in his own and was examining her forearm. Small black scars crisscrossed the underside of her arm near her wrist.

"It's like our injuries," he said, gesturing to the discolorations on his own cheek. He gently touched the marks on her skin. "How did you get these?"

Reggie's body went stiff, but she didn't pull away.

"I was cut. In Henry's fearscape. A few of the scars came back with me."

Quinn looked up at her.

"That's unbelievable. Does it hurt you?"

"Looks worse than it feels." Reggie finally tugged her arm out of Quinn's grasp. But he continued to gaze at her.

"I doubt that's true."

They stayed silent a moment, then Quinn shivered as the sun disappeared behind a cloud.

"What did you find?" she asked.

But Quinn's head jerked to the horizon, and his eyes flashed. "Shhh! Listen."

The sound of more motorcycles.

"Gale's goons. We've got to go." Quinn yanked on the other dry T-shirt and snatched up his backpack. He looked ruefully at his pants. "Damn it, wet jeans are the worst."

Reggie glanced back and forth. She wasn't keen on going anywhere more remote with Quinn, but she didn't want to run into a pack of Hell's Vours, either. She pulled her bike out from behind the bush and sat astride it.

"Come on. Get on."

Quinn squeezed onto the seat behind her, grasping her about the waist. His arms were strong, Reggie noticed, and he held her tightly. She pedaled the two of them down the path.

"Please tell me you have a place to hide," she said.

"There's a storm drain not too far up."

Reggie felt fat raindrops hit her head and arms. Quinn pointed, and she saw the tunnel at the side of the river ahead. The roar of engines grew louder. Quinn hopped off the bike as they neared the storm drain. A locked grate covered its entrance.

"What now?" said Reggie.

"Have some faith." Quinn fished a key out of his pocket and stuck it in the lock. The lock clicked and the grate swung open.

"I broke into Sewer Management one night and stole copies of their keys. I've hidden in every sewer in town at some point." Quinn held the grate open and made an after-you gesture.

"You and the rats. Appropriate," Reggie said, rolling her bike inside. Quinn relocked the grate just as the heavens opened.

Minutes later they could hear the motorcycles. They stopped on the road by the storm drain, and one biker dismounted and approached the grate, his leather jacket glistening with raindrops. Reggie and Quinn sank back into the shadowy tunnel, out of sight.

The biker tried the grate, and it clanged as he shook it back and forth, but the lock held. He looked at his companions and shrugged, then went back to his bike. Moments later, the engines gunned and faded into the distance.

Reggie heaved a sigh of relief.

"Okay, I've got to get out of here. Unlock the grate."

"I wouldn't advise that," said Quinn. "They'll circle back around a couple times trying to find us. Stay put."

"Convenient for you," said Reggie. "I had other plans this afternoon, you know."

"Consider them canceled. This is more important."

Reggie glanced at her watch. It was ten after four. There was no way she'd make it to the parole office in time, especially not in this weather.

The storm drain offered them shelter from the rain, but it wasn't comfortable. Reggie stood in ankle-deep drainage water ferrying leaves, sticks, and other debris to the river.

"So tell me what you have in that bag," she said.

Quinn pulled a packet of papers out of his backpack and held one of them up to the meager light from the storm drain's entrance. Reggie saw that it was an X-ray of sorts.

"What is it?" she asked.

"An MRI scan of a brain." He handed a series of the pages to Reggie. Some were on the X-ray film, others were colored diagrams, but all depicted images of the human brain. She shuffled through them, puzzled. This was more Aaron's field of expertise than hers.

"I don't understand what I'm looking at," she said finally.

"I don't know if I know exactly, either," said Quinn. "But I have a guess. And it's a long story."

Gusts of wind howled around the entrance as the storm raged overhead.

"Does it look like I'm going anywhere?" Reggie replied.

———※———

Aaron had to stop at home first to gather some supplies, and it was just after four when he pulled his ten-speed into the alley between the vacant convenience store and the recently relocated juvenile center. He could see rain clouds in the distance, but the sky overhead was still clear; hopefully any storm would hold off until he'd accomplished his mission. Around the corner, in the center's glass-littered parking lot, Mitch was leaning against the door of his black Crown Vic and dragging on a smoke.

Aaron thought of all the times the Kassners had tormented him — destroyed his hats, knocked books from his hands, tripped him in the halls. He always got the feeling they'd kill him for a few seconds of amusement if they thought they could get away with it. In the years Aaron had known the Kassners, he had never willingly approached either of them. Until now.

"Damn it, Reggie," he muttered under his breath, but he felt he had little choice but to do this on his own: the Kassners only met with their parole officer once a week, and waiting another seven days was out of the question.

Aaron strode across the lot with weak knees and a dry mouth. He put his right hand inside his front pocket and felt the small metal cylinder inside.

If Mitch noticed him coming, he didn't show it.

"Hey," Aaron said, barely audible.

Mitch's large head turned and he squinted, the cigarette hanging from his bottom lip.

"I — I have a question for you," Aaron squeaked.

Mitch glared coolly at Aaron, then flicked his cigarette ash at him. Aaron's legs wanted to listen and bolt, but he held firm.

"Didn't you hear?" he asked. "Smoking is bad for you."

Aaron's hand darted out, grabbed the cigarette from Mitch's lips, and threw it to the ground. Mitch was so surprised it took him a second to respond, but Aaron had already taken off toward the alley. He ran as fast as he could, as if his very life depended on it, which it probably did. Behind him he could hear the hard thumping of Mitch's steel-toed boots, gaining on him with every step. Aaron ran faster and hurtled into the alley.

He had half a second to pull the pepper spray from his pocket and turn as Mitch rounded the corner after him, red with fury. Aaron aimed and looked away, spraying Mitch full in the face as the larger boy crashed into him. They both went tumbling to the ground, Mitch crying out as he tore at his eyes. He tried to stand, and Aaron used the last of his leg strength to kick him in the groin. Mitch curled in a heap on the asphalt. Aaron collapsed against a Dumpster a few feet away, exhausted and trembling.

He glanced about nervously, but the alley was, as he had hoped, deserted. No one had seen what had happened.

His hands trembled as he took duct tape from his backpack and taped Mitch's hands behind him, then placed another strip over the boy's mouth. As soon as Mitch realized what was happening, his red and watering eyes flared with malice, but Aaron lifted the spray up in front of Mitch's face as a warning. Instead of fear, Aaron felt strangely powerful.

"I don't want to hurt you any more than this. But I swear to God I will torture the living hell out of you right here, right now if you struggle. I've got instruments packed in this bag that will make even a tough guy like you piss your pants if I use them. Do you understand me? Nod if you understand."

Mitch's eyes narrowed into wicked slits. For a moment he stayed so still that Aaron thought he'd turned to stone like some freakish gargoyle. Then slowly, deliberately, he nodded.

"Good. Now I am going to talk and you're going to listen. And when I am done talking, I'm going to take this tape off and let you answer. And then I will let you go."

Aaron jerked on one of his shoulder straps to let Mitch hear the sounds of cold metal clanging together inside the pack.

"But if I think for a second that you're coming after me, I will cut you open and toss you in the Dumpster for the rats. Nod if you understand."

Again, a long pause. And another nod.

"Good. Now what I am going to say would sound crazy to most people. But I'm betting it won't sound crazy to you. I think you've lived through it. I think you know all about it. I think you know all about what's happened to your brother."

Mitch's bleary eyes opened a little wider. Aaron saw a flicker of alarm, but he continued.

"Keech isn't human, is he? His body was possessed by some kind of demon. That thing inside talking to your probation officer looks like Keech and acts like Keech, but it isn't him. And you know it, don't you?"

Mitch's whole body tensed, and he looked away. He made no noise, but Aaron sensed an internal struggle inside that meathead.

"Mitch. I want to help," he said.

Mitch finally gazed up at him, and Aaron saw the last thing he expected. In those haunted eyes was sadness. Guilt.

And terror.

Aaron slowly reached for the tape covering Mitch's mouth.

"When I take this off, you are going to tell me what you know. But if you make any sudden moves, I will hurt you. Bad."

Aaron pulled the corner of the tape, the moist and sticky adhesive stretching the stubbly skin beneath. It must have hurt, but Mitch's expression registered no physical pain.

He opened his mouth, and the words tumbled out, as if they had been locked up behind those lips for years.

"Eight years ago. Three days before Christmas," Mitch said. "He disappeared. Something came for him at night. I heard him crying and screaming. I thought it was just another nightmare — he always had those. But this was different. The bedroom froze. I could hear ice cracking on the ceiling. I never saw anything, but I could feel it."

Mitch glanced down and wet his lips. Aaron realized with some wonder that he'd never actually heard Mitch speak before — Keech always did the talking for the both of them. But where Keech always sounded harsh and cruel, Mitch's voice was soft, quiet, and strangely, almost sensitive. Aaron grasped for the first time what horrors the older twin must have lived with for so long, and where before there had been only anger, now he felt pity for the guy who had so often tormented him.

"They're called Vours, Mitch. They prey on the weak and the frightened. Mostly children —"

"I know what they are, Cole. That thing that took my brother made sure I knew. " Mitch's eyes, irritated and red from the spray, darted around. "Every day I wish I didn't."

"It's messed with your mind. Shown you your fears, and scared the shit out of you."

Mitch nodded.

"How do you know these things?" Mitch asked.

"They've done it to me, too."

Mitch's agitated eyes started to glisten.

"Every night. Every single night." With his hands taped behind him, Mitch tried to wipe tears away with his shoulder. Aaron took a breath, then undid the tape. He grimaced as he saw that he had wrapped it so tightly, it had cut into Mitch's skin, leaving slim red welts. Mitch rubbed his wrists.

"That thing that lives in your brother's body. What does it want?"

"To hurt. To destroy. That's what it wants. That's all it ever wants."

"Has it ever tried to kill you?"

Mitch shook his head. "What fun would that be for it? Plus I'm its protector from the hunters."

Aaron leaned forward.

"Hunters? What hunters?"

Mitch shrugged. "One came after us a few years ago."

"And where is he now?"

"She." Mitch looked away. "Dead."

"Keech killed her?" Aaron remembered hearing the whispers when the twins first moved to Cutter's Wedge that they had killed someone, but he had always chalked it up to the high school's overactive rumor mill.

"No. Keech didn't."

Finally Aaron understood. The monster had used a human to do its dirty work. Mitch had been its instrument.

"I'm sorry. I'm so . . . sorry."

Mitch sniffed.

"The things I've already done, I know when I die I'll go to hell, but there's no way it could be worse than this life."

He grabbed the side of the Dumpster and pulled himself up. He looked cowed now, not like the bully everyone feared.

"You shouldn't have gotten mixed up in this, Cole. You are as good as dead. We both are." He sighed. "Maybe it's better that way."

"I know how to stop them, Mitch."

"You want me to kill him. That it?" Mucus rolled from Mitch's nostrils and over his top lip. "Some nights when it sleeps, I think about it. I picture myself strangling it in bed. Stabbing it to death. Lighting it on fire and watching it burn and listening to it howl. I've seen it do that to animals. Some days I would rather fry in the chair than live with that thing. But I can't do it. I can't kill my brother."

Aaron scrambled to his feet.

"We don't have to kill him. There's a way to save him."

Mitch's puffy, red eyes locked with Aaron's.

"If you are lying, Cole, you better just kill me now. Screw with me about this and I will rip you apart. I don't care what you've got in that pack, it won't be enough to save your ass."

"I'm telling you the truth. But the only way we can save him is if I have your help. There's no way I could overpower him alone. And if we're going to find the real Keech, we'll need to make the Vour vulnerable."

"Cold."

"Yeah, exactly. Does it still affect him?"

"It does weird things to its skin. It was a lot worse when we were younger, but it still hates it. Makes it weak."

"Good. That's important for this to work."

"So you want me to lure it somewhere cold and trap it for you? Maybe I could do it. Then what?"

"If I tried to explain it to you now, you wouldn't understand. Hell, I don't even understand it. All you need to know is that I have a friend who can bring your brother back."

"The Halloway chick."

"Reggie. Her name is Reggie. The girl you tried to kill."

Mitch closed his eyes.

"I didn't want any part of that," he said. "But it gets to the point when you'll do anything to make the nightmares stop."

"I know."

"Keech is extra careful these days because of her. Won't tell me why, but he's definitely bugged about her."

Mitch took two steps forward and towered over Aaron, looking down at him menacingly.

"Give me your cell."

"What?"

"Your number. I'll get him someplace cold. And when I do, I'll call you."

"When?"

"When I can. Be ready. You and your girl."

"Where —"

"Just give me the number and shut up." Mitch wiped his eyes and squinted into the morning sun. "I've got ten minutes before I meet with my probe. And if Keech sees you here, you're done. So get the hell out and wait for my call."

Aaron nodded, scratched his number down on a piece of notebook paper and handed it to Mitch. Then he grabbed his bike from the other side of the Dumpster.

"And Cole?" Mitch spoke without turning around. "This doesn't make us friends. You touch me again, I'll kill you."

Aaron pedaled off toward Something Wicked just as the first sprinkles of rain began to dot the asphalt.

The harmless spoons and forks in his backpack jingled with every bump in the cracked pavement.

11

Quinn leaned back against the wall of the storm drain.

"Vours have existed for, well, forever, as far as any of us knows. I've lived in many different bodies before this one. Let me see . . . I've been an ancient Sumerian, a Renaissance architect, a fifties beatnik. The Dark Ages were the worst. I *never* want to repeat that experience. But the point is, no one, neither human nor Vour, really knows where we came from, how we come into existence, or how we're able to take over bodies on Sorry Night. We know we can, but we don't know why or how the process works. You've asked the question before, Halloway — what do the Vours want? Well, above all things, for centuries and centuries, we've wanted the answers to those questions. If we knew those things, there'd be no stopping us."

Quinn paused as the roar of the motorcycles passed by once again, then faded into the distance.

"For ages, the answers seemed to lie in mysticism. Black and white magic — mostly black — faith, religion, devil worship, spells — all that bunk. We didn't know any better. Our sciences were the same as yours. Some of the greatest scientists and religious leaders in history were Vours trying to figure things out. Rasputin was one of the most infamous — not that he did a very good job disguising what he was."

"You make it sound so benign," said Reggie. "Like doctors trying to find a cure for cancer."

"That's a good analogy. To us, humans *are* the cancer."

Reggie bristled.

"Hello, you possess us, remember? Like parasites."

"Do you want to know this stuff or not? I'm just telling you like it is," Quinn shot back. When Reggie was silent, he went on. "So yeah, it wasn't until the last century or so that we started to look at more concrete possibilities. The human brain is a more complex machine than anything else in existence. Scientists started to theorize that Vours and humans were connected physically, *chemically*, and not just psychically. So they started to look at the brain, its parts, its functions."

"And what did they find?" Reggie asked.

"The amygdala."

At Reggie's questioning look, Quinn pointed to two red spots in the center of one of the brain images.

"They're neuron hives that help humans identify and remember emotions, particularly fear. When you're afraid of something, it's because your amygdala is sending signals registering fear to all the corners of your body. Sweaty palms, shallow breaths, goosebumps — all responses triggered by the amygdala. It remembers fear, and it tells your body how to react."

"But what does that have to do with Vours?"

"As far as we can tell, our world is some other plane of existence from this one, like another dimension. Somehow, only on Sorry Night, we're able to cross over into this dimension. How? What's the popular sci-fi explanation for traveling between dimensions?"

"I don't know. Wormholes. Gateways —"

"Bingo. A gateway. But it needn't be a physical door. What if the gateway is something in the human brain, something that neurologically links the Vour world and the human world? Fear, after all, is just a series of nerve impulses caused by these neuron groupings. The amygdala is the key — *it*'s the gateway."

Reggie squinted at Quinn.

"So you're saying that all this Vour research has proved that you monsters enter us through our own brains? That does sound like science fiction."

Quinn chuckled.

"And I suppose when your brother was taken over and sent to a fearscape, you thought it was rationally explainable? Come on, Reggie, you know there have to be alternative theories about these things. The beauty of this one is that it's not rooted in witchcraft or voodoo or original sin or anything like that. It's letting science guide the way to the answer."

"But what does Sorry Night have to do with it?"

"That was the stumbling block. I didn't even realize they'd hit on it until I found these. New advances in their equipment have yielded better studies and pictures of the amygdala — look here."

Quinn started flipping through some of the brain scans. A label at the top read "Patient B137."

"So you can see these are all pictures of the same brain, right?"

Reggie nodded.

"Check out the time stamps."

Reggie took the scans and examined the dates printed in the corner of each: June 21, Aug 13, Oct 31, Dec 21, Feb 27, Apr 16. In the June picture, the red dots were small and faint, but as they progressed through the summer and into fall and winter, they grew in size and intensity. Then as winter passed to spring, they started to shrink again. According to the images, Patient B137's amygdala was at its largest on Dec 21, the night of the winter solstice. Sorry Night.

"Why would the time of year matter to the amygdala's size?" she asked Quinn.

"Don't ask me — I needed tutoring in biology," he replied. "Maybe it has to do with circadian rhythms or something like that, or something not yet explainable by today's science. The point is, the Vours think this is the key. Look at these."

Quinn handed over a few more MRIs, all of different patients. But they were unlike B137's. L52's amygdala was comparatively large for an April 5 scan, while R255's was tiny on Dec 16.

"What does this mean?" Reggie asked. "They found exceptions to the rule?"

"Or they *created* exceptions to the rule."

Reggie caught her breath.

"You mean like . . . experiments?"

Quinn took the scans from Reggie and put them back into his bag.

"I told you — lots of scientists in history have been Vours.

And let's just say they don't have too many ethical qualms when it comes to human testing. What these pictures tell me is that the Vours think the size of the amygdala is the key to us being able to take over humans. Now they're trying to artificially enlarge them, so that we can come through any day of the year, not just Sorry Night."

"How are they enlarging them?"

"I don't know, but I don't envy whoever they're doing it to. Knowing my old kindred, I'd guess it'd have to do with injecting them with various concoctions, feeding them things, giving them hallucinations —"

"Okay, stop, I get the picture. But it obviously hasn't worked yet, since we're not all walking around as Vours."

"Given their current spree to get rid of the two of us, I'd say they're close to discovering the answer. The summer solstice is days away — if they can make this work on that day, when we're usually at our weakest . . ."

Reggie blew out a slow breath. Aaron was always talking about how humans used such a tiny percentage of their brains, that skills like ESP and telekinesis could be achieved if people could just learn how to access those parts of the mind. Maybe the brain was also home to darker things, more evil things . . .

"How can we stop it?"

"We have to find them, first," Quinn said. "Wherever they've set up shop, I don't know about it."

Lightning flashed, and thunder growled like a giant's belly. They were silent as they heard the bikes pass by again. Reggie began to pace.

"Don't you have any idea where they might be? Any old haunts? Can't you sniff them out or something?"

"What do you think I've been doing the past several days? They've gone underground. But look, they're doing medical experiments. That means a place with equipment, labs, technicians. Maybe a clinic? Or a hospital? I don't know how we'd search out every doctor's office in the area by next week, but it's a place to start."

Reggie stopped pacing.

"A mental hospital," she said.

"What's that?" Quinn asked.

"They're studying brains — it could be a mental hospital." Reggie felt her knees weak beneath her. "Oh, God. *Thornwood.*"

"What?"

"Where Henry goes, where his shrink works." She raced to the grate and pulled on it, but Quinn caught her arm and held her back.

"No way, they're still out there."

"I need to see my brother."

"Is he at Thornwood right now?"

Reggie's mind was racing, and it took her a minute to think of the right answer to the question. It was Friday afternoon; no, Henry saw Unger on Thursdays now.

"No."

"Then you don't need to save him from anything right this second. Chill. Let's think this through."

Reggie paced again.

"Thornwood would be the perfect place for the Vours. It's a private hospital, out in the middle of nowhere."

"It could be the place. Just make sure Henry doesn't go back there until we check it out."

"No kidding."

The trees thrashed and waved in the gusts. Neither of them said anything for several minutes. Quinn squatted by the wall, resting his back on it. Reggie eyed him warily.

"Why are you doing this? Why do *you* want to stop this from happening? Open bodies twenty-four seven — sounds like your dream come true."

Quinn stuck his hand back in his bag and pulled out two purple lollipops.

"I just like these too much."

He held one out to Reggie, but she shook her head, so he unwrapped them and popped both in his mouth.

"Our world is a void of nothingness — no warmth, no sugar, no fun stuff." He sucked on the lollipop for a minute, savoring the sweet flavor. "The truth is, if there were a revolving door between this world and ours, I think we'd fuck it all up over here. We'd turn here into there. We'd lose everything that we crave."

"And we wouldn't want *that*," Reggie said.

Quinn stood and looked thoughtfully at her.

"You know, Halloway, I think you like having me around."

Reggie's eyes flashed.

"Sorry. Demons aren't my type."

"Right, so geeky guys who follow you like puppy dogs are more your style? I don't think so. What does Mr. Unrequited have to say about me, anyway? I'm surprised I haven't seen him around, armed with a lead pipe and a shovel."

Reggie flushed.

"Leave Aaron out of this."

The corners of Quinn's mouth lifted into a sly grin.

"Wait. You didn't tell him, did you?"

"After what he's been through — this would distract him from the big picture."

"So you put him on a need-to-know basis. I like this side of you, Halloway. It's so . . . devious."

"He would kill you if he knew you were still alive."

"I think you just want me for yourself."

Quinn stepped closer to Reggie, and she could smell his sweet breath. She was reminded of the first day she spoke to him in the hall at school. Her heart had pounded in her chest then, and it was pounding now. The gash beneath his eye had started to heal, but there would always be a scar, as well as the black crisscrosses down his cheek. Yet somehow, he wasn't hideous. He'd lost his conventional looks undoubtedly, but they'd been replaced with something striking and dark. His exterior matched his true self now, the Vour self, and Reggie realized she found that refreshing. It was honest. There was no more pretense between them, no walls, no masks. It was both a relief and a terror.

She turned her head away.

"You went through hell and lived," Quinn said softly. "That leaves marks." He lifted her forearm and lightly touched her skin. "Marks deeper than these."

"They'll heal," Reggie said.

"Why don't you just ask me what you've been dying to know ever since I showed up in your bedroom?"

"And what's that?"

"What it's like in the darkness. I'm the only one who understands what you've lived through. What you're living with now."

Reggie pulled away, but Quinn continued.

"You feel a shadow around you. Inside you. Growing. And it terrifies you. I know what you fear most, Reggie."

"Stop . . ."

"Turning into one of us."

Reggie stepped back, and now she was pressed against the wall. Quinn drew nearer so that he loomed over her. She could feel his lean but strong body against her own, and she wondered if he noticed how hard she was breathing.

He raised his hand and drew it gently down her cheek. Reggie felt tears springing up and tried to look away, but Quinn turned her chin upward so that his eyes were looking down into hers.

"The darkness gives you power," he murmured. His colorless lips were inches from her own. "More power than any human. Don't deny it. *Use it*. You and I are more alike than you think."

Reggie shuddered and pushed him back.

"I will never be like you," she said through gritted teeth. "You disgust me." She ran to the edge of the storm drain. The clouds seemed to be clearing up and the rain had slowed to a drizzle. She hadn't heard the motorcycles in some time. She pulled on the grate; it clanged back and forth but held fast. "Unlock it."

Without another word, Quinn unlocked the gate and swung it open. Reggie dragged her bike out of the storm drain, and Quinn watched her silently as she sped down the path toward town.

12

Reggie found Henry playing in his room when she got home. She strode through his door and wrapped her arms around him in a great bear hug.

"Reggie, that hurts," Henry complained.

"Sorry. I was just worried."

"Why? I'm fine."

Reggie sat down next to him on the floor.

"Henry, you know how you told me the other night that you got that funny feeling, like the heat was being sucked out of you?"

"Uh-huh."

"Have you ever gotten that feeling before?"

Henry thought for a moment.

"I don't think so."

"You've never felt it when you were at Thornwood? Or with Dr. Unger?"

Henry shook his head.

"No. Why?"

Reggie sighed. It was comforting that her brother hadn't expressly felt the Vours' presence at the hospital, but it wasn't proof positive that they hadn't infiltrated it. She wasn't sure when this ability of his had developed; maybe it was something relatively new.

"Henry, you can't go to Thornwood anymore. It's too dangerous."

Henry's eyes narrowed.

"What happened?"

"Nothing yet. I just found some things out — Vours might be at Thornwood."

"What?" Henry started backward, knocking over a toy pirate ship. The pieces scattered everywhere.

"No, I don't want you to be scared!" Reggie insisted. Internally she swore at herself for dumping such information on him so casually. "It's just something I heard. Maybe it's not true, but it's too risky. I'm going to talk to Dad — I'll make up some excuse why you can't go there anymore. I'm sorry, Hen — I know Dr. Unger was helping you. We'll find you someone else really good."

Reggie began gathering up the plastic pieces of ship.

"Why did you think I felt those things when I was at Thornwood?" Henry asked.

Reggie sat up on her heels.

"What?"

"My heat being sucked out. Why would that happen at Thornwood?"

Reggie hesitated. She worried that if Henry did have an internal Vour detector, it might freak him out too badly to know about it. Sometimes not knowing Vours could be anyone around you was a blessing.

"I want you to tell me what it is," Henry said. "I'm not a baby. I won't be afraid."

Reggie knelt back down on the floor.

"I know you're not a baby, Hen. But these are really scary things, and I don't want you to have to deal with them."

"But I'm already dealing with them. Sometimes I don't even know what's real anymore."

Reggie bit her thumbnail.

"I know. I'm so sorry —"

"Don't be sorry," Henry said. "Everyone's always sorry. That doesn't do any good. I want to know what's happening to me."

"Henry —"

"Am I turning back into a Vour?"

"What?" Reggie jerked her head up.

"Is my heat going away because I'm turning back into a Vour?"

"God — no!" Reggie pulled him into a hug, but he remained still. "No, that's not it at all. Don't ever think that!"

Henry's face was resolute, but he was breathing fast, and his lips trembled.

"Well, what then?" he asked.

"It's just . . . okay." Reggie sat back, keeping her gaze even with Henry's. "Look, we're not totally positive or anything, but Aaron and I were thinking that . . . maybe that feeling you get is a sign . . . a sign that Vours are nearby. Like a warning. It gets stronger when they're closer."

"But it happened the other night in our house!"

"I know," Reggie said quickly. "There must have been a Vour outside someplace, and you sensed it."

"Oh my gosh." Terror flitted across Henry's face, but he stayed calm.

"Don't worry, Henry," Reggie went on. She stroked the side of his head. "There's nothing wrong with you. If anything, this is a good thing. It will help you avoid Vours."

Henry shook his head.

"But if you think there are Vours at Thornwood, wouldn't I have felt them already?"

"It might not be that simple. Maybe it's still developing. Maybe you just haven't felt them there *yet*. But that's why I don't want you to go back."

Henry pulled his knees up to his chin and sat huddled like that for several minutes, pensive and silent. Reggie watched him anxiously.

"I shouldn't have told you," she said. "It's so much to handle, and after everything you've already been through —"

"I can try it out Tuesday." Henry looked up at her. "Dad told me we're all supposed to go for another family session, and he's going to make you come."

"What? No. No way. I don't want you anywhere near that place. And if you ever get that feeling again, I want you to run."

"I'm tired of being scared," Henry said softly. "I was always running in the fearscape, running away from the scary things." He stood up and put his hand on Reggie's shoulder. "You made me face them, remember? That's how we got out. That's what we should do now."

"Henry, you shouldn't be involved in this."

"Why not? Because I'm younger than you? I've seen the same

things. And now I want to fight back. So we're going to Thorn-wood on Tuesday."

Henry crossed his arms and stared sternly at Reggie. She was surprised to see the same look her mother used to give her when she was serious about something.

It was actually a good plan, one that could possibly save her a lot of time. Both she and her father would be there; Henry wouldn't really be in any unnecessary danger. More than anything she was astonished at his resolve, his courage. She had no right to dictate what he could and couldn't do — he'd beaten a fearscape, after all.

"Tuesday?"

"At ten."

"Let's do it."

* * *

Aaron had kept his phone on and by his pillow all night in case Mitch called, but he had heard nothing more from him by morning. Though technically the first day of summer break, Aaron rose early and headed to Something Wicked; he had to open the shop this morning since Eben had errands to run in Fredericks. Aaron suspected those errands involved Vours, but Eben stonewalled him every time he asked. If Aaron was to learn anything about Eben's connection to these monsters, he was going to have to find out in more secretive ways.

One of the things Aaron liked most about working for Eben was that his boss didn't believe in busywork. Once the Internet orders were packed and shipped (all two of them), the incoming books received and shelved, Aaron was free to read. Every shift he dusted off old pulps, horror reprints, science texts, and horror history books. In the past six months, both at home and at work, he had obsessively researched monster lore of all kinds. Before Sorry Night Aaron had always preferred true crime — before the fairy-tale nightmares called the Vours became true stories themselves.

Today, Aaron spent the hours combing through volume after volume, determined to unearth something useful about the monsters and what link existed between them and the solstices. Even if the answer lay in myth, it would be a place to start. But the going was slow, and he found very little to help him.

The bookstore was like a cave, dark and cool, the air-conditioning turned up high to help preserve the aging tomes. Normally Aaron appreciated the atmosphere, especially compared to the sweltering summer outside, but now, alone amid the scent of old paper and mustiness, his memories of the Vour in his head closed in on him. Focusing on his research and on how he could help Reggie was the only thing that kept the mania at bay. Time was running out.

Right up until closing he scoured *Unspeakable Cults* but found more of the same trite tales — accounts of demented charlatans, demon worshippers, and dark spirit conjurers, but nothing shed further light on the secrets of the Vours.

The bell above the door chimed just before seven o'clock. Eben knocked dirt from his shoes with his cane and stepped inside. It bothered Aaron that Eben still used the cane, now that he'd witnessed just how capable he really was. Sometimes when he closed his eyes, Aaron still heard the sickening crack of Quinn's wrist moments before Eben let the monster sink into the freezing lake. He locked the door and flipped the sign over in the window.

There was much to fear about the old man. But deep down, Aaron knew they needed him, even if Reggie refused to believe it.

"Find any first edition Poes today, boss? Can we retire rich?"

He slid the book beneath the counter behind the register.

"Nothing but junk today. Though the drive was rather pleasant. So much green this time of year."

Eben walked behind the counter and hung up his hat. He eyed the title of the book beneath the register and shook his head in disappointment. "After all you've been through, you're still sticking your nose where it can get chopped off? Let it go, boy."

"Believe me, I want to." Aaron followed Eben to the register. "Are you going to tell me what you did to that detective to get me out of jail?"

"No."

"Candy? Flowers?"

"Enough. I've warned you too often." Eben glared at Aaron. "But you're not the only one I should be warning, am I right?"

Aaron said nothing. The old man leaned toward him, his gray eyes boring into the boy's own.

"What does she mean to do?"

"I don't know."

"I need you to tell me."

"Eben, I don't know anything."

"You're a bad liar, boy. If you let her get in harm's way again, could you live with yourself? Tell me what she's planning."

Aaron bit his lip. He made a decision.

"There's a Vour at school. He came after her the other day. Reggie didn't want me to tell you, but I trust you can listen and not flip out."

Eben clutched Aaron's shoulder. His fingers tensed like a clamp. Aaron pulled away, startled by the elderly man's grip.

"Or maybe not."

"Why didn't you tell me?"

"She thinks she can save him."

The color drained from Eben's face. "And what do you think?"

"I think she's braver than all of us."

"She's a fool. You're both fools."

"Look, I'm not saying I agree with her, but —"

"Then convince her that this path is reckless — worse, down-right idiotic! It's suicide!"

"Don't you think I've told her this, Eben?" said Aaron. "It doesn't matter. Reggie is the hero in this story, no matter what you and I think." Eben glared at him icily. Aaron could feel his pulse quickening. "Did you ever ask yourself, why her? It's because she's just better than us. She chooses to fight, to save the victim, at risk to herself. I don't like it — I hate it! But it's what makes her the perfect one to fight the Vours. And there's nothing you or I can do about it except watch her back!"

Eben slapped Aaron across the face. Aaron staggered back, cupping his cheek in shock.

"This isn't one of your novels!" Eben shouted at him. "The villain can't be vanquished, and the hero won't win!" He grabbed Aaron by the collar. "There are fates far worse than mortal death. Do you understand? I will not let her risk a suffering beyond human understanding for the slim hope of saving strangers! Would you? Would you let her *soul* die for this?"

Aaron ripped himself free from the old man's white-knuckled grip and pushed him hard in the chest. Eben stumbled backward, tripped on a box of books, and fell. A dull crack pierced the air as Eben struck the wooden floor.

Protruding from the thin, liver-spotted skin on Eben's wrist was bone, blackened and brittle, like a chicken wing left to burn in an oven. Droplets of dark blood seeped from the wound.

"Eben!"

Then the man convulsed and broke into a horrific coughing spasm. He gasped for breath but choked on a wetness building in his throat and lungs. His eyes widened and he tried to stand, but a stream of red and gray ooze poured from his mouth and nostrils.

Aaron stood, frozen in shock and disgust.

Eben extended his broken arm upward and hacked, noxious fluid spraying from his mouth. Aaron snatched the phone from the counter and dialed 9-1-1 while he knelt and cradled Eben's head. The emergency operator picked up on the first ring.

"Send an ambulance! My boss —"

"No! Aaron!" Eben gurgled, slapping at the phone.

"My boss collapsed. There's blood . . ."

"Please . . . don't . . ."

"The Something Wicked bookstore on Main. Send someone. Please, send them *now*."

Aaron dropped the phone and lifted Eben into an upright position, hoping to ease his coughing. He tried not to look, but his eyes moved involuntarily to the diseased bone sticking out of the man's wrist.

It was gruesome and unnatural. Repulsive.

The coughing continued, though Eben's breath now drew a bit easier and the flow of bloody toxins from his mouth and nose slowed to a trickle.

"Eben. I'm so sorry . . ."

Eben closed his eyes and shook his head, pained by something much greater than his physical injuries.

"It's all over now. I am found out."

13

Reggie raced into the Cutter's Wedge Emergency Room lobby. The place smelled like an infected wound soaked in bleach. When Aaron had called her and told her about Eben, all of her anger had turned to worry for the man she had once loved like a second father.

Reggie pressed her palms against the cool marble counter. The clerk on the opposite side had thin wisps of yellowish gray hair and thick glasses that made his brown eyes look cartoonish.

"Can I help you?"

"Where is Eben Bloch? An ambulance brought him in —"

Aaron's long fingers clutched her arm. "Come on, he's on the third floor."

They moved quickly to an open elevator and dashed inside as the doors closed. Fluorescent bulbs lit the small space, and canned music played from the speakers. Shivers erupted over Reggie's skin as the tune summoned up the hospital images from her brother's fearscape in her head: the demon infants, the cancerous ghosts of dead children, the monstrous surgeon — all of the visceral horrors from her memories pressed down upon her. She felt the acidic burn of the surgeon's needle in her neck, the bites of the fanged baby zombies in her calves and thighs . . .

"Reggie? You okay?"

"Yeah," she said. "I just don't like hospitals."

Aaron took her hand and held it until they stopped on the third floor and the doors dinged opened again.

They approached the nurse's station, where a young woman sat and scribbled onto one of many medical charts stacked beside her.

"Hi," Aaron said nervously. "We're here to see Eben Bloch?"

The nurse shook her head and stood up.

"Dr. Kwan wants him to rest. No visitors for the evening. Perhaps first thing in the morning? I'm sorry."

"But I'm his daughter," Reggie lied. Aaron said nothing.

The nurse shuffled through her charts and examined one closely.

"This says Mr. Bloch has no immediate family."

"We've been — estranged," Reggie stammered. "Please. I'm all he's got."

The nurse looked around furtively, put down her clipboard and then stepped out from behind the station. She looked to Aaron.

"You will need to stay here."

Aaron nodded respectfully.

"Thank you," Reggie squeezed Aaron's hand.

"Take your time. I'll be here."

Reggie drew a deep breath and followed the nurse down the hall and around a corner to the farthest room in the unit. Outside the door the nursed stopped and turned.

"Put these on." She handed Reggie a mask and a pair of latex gloves. "Do not take them off for any reason. Dr. Kwan may decide to quarantine your father if the tests come back and cause concern. We haven't . . ." The nurse struggled. "I've never seen these symptoms in a patient before. I don't mean to frighten you by saying that, it's just —"

"I understand." Reggie tied the mask behind her head and pulled the gloves on her hands. "I'm not afraid."

The nurse nodded and left Reggie at the door. She stepped into the room, which seemed more like a cell than a hospital suite. The throb of beeping machines and labored breaths filled the air. From behind an olive green curtain a choked voice called out, "Aaron?"

"No, it's Reggie." Her speech sounded thin in the sterilized room, and she realized she was terrified to face Eben here, alone. She heard his ragged breaths and winced behind her mask.

"Ah, Regina. You see the lengths I have to go to get you to visit me."

"Aaron called me. He told me you were . . . sick." The machines hissed and whirred. Reggie stood before the curtain and looked down at the chipped linoleum tiles. "What's happening to you, Eben? The nurse said —"

Hollow coughs interrupted her.

"Oh, I doubt the nurse, or the doctor, or a team of scientists could diagnose this," Eben rasped. "There are things I need to tell you, Regina. Pull back the curtain. Go ahead. It's okay."

Reggie fingered the sickly green drapery, then pulled it aside, scraping the rings along their metal rod. Behind it, a ruined Eben Bloch stared up from the hospital bed. Reggie, who had never seen him in short sleeves before, saw that the man's thin arms were not only ropy with muscle, but also pitted and criss-crossed with scars. He looked like the living dead.

Any anger toward him left in her evaporated at the sight of his pallid form. Various tubes and wires ran from his arms and chest, and his wrist was wrapped in a thick cast. Medical equipment stood over his bed. He'd hidden what he'd known about the Vours from her, even after they'd taken over Henry, but for a time he'd been so dear to her — and in the end he'd saved her life. And Henry's. A desperate sadness rose up in place of her bitterness.

"Please don't die," she pleaded.

"That may not be up to me," Eben said. "And you need to know the truth, before it's too late."

He motioned her closer. Reggie rolled the doctor's stool over to him and sat down.

"It happened to me, too," he said. "They took my own sister away, like they did to Henry. But I never got her back."

Reggie put her hand on his shoulder.

"You don't need to do this now. Not when you're sick."

"Yes, I do." He coughed. "We believed in Sorry Night where I grew up, too. Only our village called it Kracun. In stories, it was supposed to be the day evil spirits returned to the earth."

Reggie wondered if he was delirious from illness. Eben caught her expression. His gaze cleared and his breathing became steadier.

"When I was a boy, on the night of the winter solstice, we'd light fires in the crossroads and graveyards on the edge of town. Legend said that it warmed the ghosts, but —"

"It drew the Vours away from people," Reggie said quietly. "They'd follow the heat and light."

Eben grunted his affirmation. "We'd snuff the lamps and hide in the darkness and cold, huddled together and praying for morning. For years, it passed as just another local tradition to me, a superstition. Then it all changed."

Eben looked past Reggie, as if trying to remember.

"One year, my older sister Alanna went hunting on the solstice. It had been a harsh winter, and we were starving. Alanna was a crack shot, better than most of the men. She left at dawn, but by noon, a blizzard had rolled in, and at sunset, she still hadn't returned." Eben took a ragged breath. "People were too frightened of the ghosts to search for her. My father told me that Alanna would see the lights of the bonfires outside of town, and they would lead her home. So I prayed all night for my sister's return. She never came back."

"But something that looked like her did?"

Eben's head nodded ever so slightly.

"Alanna rode back to us the next morning, but she had changed. She was no longer good-hearted and brave, joyful and funny. She had turned cruel. Gluttonous. She was wise in a terrible way, a witch who knew what everyone feared. I lived in her shadow for years — I endured terrors and visions. So, when I was the same age you are now, I . . ." Eben's voice was unnervingly calm now. "I freed her. She took me to the forest to chop wood to keep the fire going, and I carried the axe. And in that forest I freed Alanna from the Vour. Do you understand?"

"Yes."

"Everyone knew what I had done, and they brought me before the village council. I was sure I would be hanged. Instead, they put me on a carriage and sent me away. Then I was put on a train, then a boat. It seemed they were going to send me to the end of the Earth. But once there, I was taught to be a Tracer."

"A what? Tracer?"

"For centuries Tracers have tracked the Vours, freeing their victims the only way we know how. We have never questioned what must be done . . . until now."

Reggie was stunned. "Do the Tracers still exist?"

"Yes." Eben shrugged. "But how many? Where? This is not for me to know. I'm just a soldier."

A nurse peeked in the window. Eben waved her away.

"Why are you telling me this now?" Reggie asked.

"Aaron said something to me today. It made me angry, but he was right. You've chosen to fight, just as I had chosen so many years ago. But your power is something this world has never seen. You are a new breed of soldier, Regina. And I fear your fight will cost you dearly before it is done."

Reggie gripped the bed rail as Eben continued.

"When an infected human dies, the Vour essence seeps out before disappearing. Whether it's destroyed or gone back to its own world, we don't know, but that substance, what we see as smoke, is an evil cancer of unknown origin. I've killed hundreds of Vours in my time, and who knows how much poison I've absorbed. It has taken my lungs, surged through my veins, charred my bones —" He took a handkerchief from the bedside table and coughed into it, then held it up for Reggie to see. Black spittle spotted the whiteness. "This is who I've become."

Eben folded the handkerchief neatly in squares and placed it back on the table. Reggie thought of the smoke that had come from Detective Gale's body, and she hoped the mask she wore hid the horror she felt.

"I didn't know," she said.

"I didn't want you to," Eben replied. "This is the curse of the Tracer, at least those who live long enough. A black virus that slowly eats away our insides is the punishment for the life we lead, for the sins we commit on behalf of a greater good."

"But I don't need to fight them the way you have," Reggie insisted. "There's another way now."

"Yes, and I imagine your method is all the more dangerous. If a Vour essence can do this to me in this world, what must be happening to you when you trespass into theirs?" He pointed to his scars. "I fear your future will be much worse."

Reggie tried to swallow the lump forming in her throat. The nurse came in again, and this time Eben could not wave her away.

"I'm sorry dear, but it's time for your father to sleep. You can come back tomorrow."

Reggie put her hand on Eben's.

"I will. I'll come back tomorrow."

The nurse had injected something into Eben's IV bag, and already his eyelids were drooping. Reggie stayed until she felt his hand go limp, and his breathing slowed. She went back into the hall and the nurse followed, clicking off the lights and shutting the door behind them.

Aaron was just flipping his phone closed as Reggie got back to the waiting area.

"Perfect timing. That was Mitch. We're on."

14

Aaron and Reggie dropped their bikes behind the football field bleachers and walked the two hundred yards to the school. The sun had gone down, and mosquitoes swarmed them in search of moist skin and fresh blood. Both walked wide circles around the pale pools of light cast by the humming floodlights that illuminated pockets of brick along the building. The school looked like a prison in the night, harsh and secretive.

Aaron spotted the broken window first.

"There. Principal's office. Figures."

He scuttled across the sprinkler-soaked grass in an awkward crouch. Reggie followed.

"No alarms?"

"No. But after tonight?" Aaron pulled two sets of latex gloves from his backpack and handed a pair to Reggie. Then he took a flashlight out and used it to brush away the glass teeth that protruded from the side and bottom edges of the pane. "This will be the Kassners' last break-in, I think. Don't cut yourself, Reg."

Aaron slipped in through the window, stepped onto the air-conditioning unit that lined the back wall of the room, and hopped to the floor. He offered up a hand to guide Reggie down into the office. Even in the relative dark, she sensed the carnage first. She could smell it.

Formaldehyde.

She snatched the flashlight from Aaron and scanned the room with the ghostly beam of light. Lab animals had been strewn across the floor, some of them torn into pulpy pieces. Two headless rat bodies littered Principal Padian's oak desk, and blood had been smeared across the family pictures that adorned each corner. In the pen cup, the decapitated heads of the rodents were punctured atop the tips of fine custom pens. A dissected frog was pierced into the back of the leather chair with yellow and blue pushpins. There was nothing ritualistic or sacrificial about any of the butchery, nothing to suggest that the bloody mess had any purpose. It was simple and brutal cruelty.

"Keech." The scene reminded Reggie too much of what Henry's Vour had done to his pet hamster.

Aaron observed the dead creatures with a cool distance but said nothing. The killer or killers had taken their time. They had enjoyed themselves.

"Let's go, Reggie. And don't touch anything. Nothing we can do here."

Reggie walked ahead down the dark hall. It was a mine of destruction: every glass case shattered, every art piece thrown to the tile floor and smashed. When the Vour inside Henry terrorized her last winter, the film of fear had blunted her anger. But now with each step down the trashed school hall, her blood pumped harder and hotter at this recklessness.

First, the monster had violated her home, her family. And

now it spilled its malice across the rest of her life in Cutter's Wedge, and its evil wreckage marked the deterioration of her own fear and empathy. She stalked into the dark cafeteria toward the double doors that lead into the kitchen.

"Yo."

A hulking figure stepped out from the shadows and stood right in front of the doors.

"I wondered if you'd show."

Reggie stopped and thrust the flashlight beam into the large boy's face. He'd been beaten. His bottom lip bled freely; his right eye was swollen. He smiled to reveal blood-caked teeth.

"Where is he, Mitch?" Aaron asked. "Where's Keech?"

"Where I said he'd be. Kicked my ass a little, but I got him." The boy wiped his lip and rubbed the blood between his thumb and forefinger. "Don't know how much longer he'll last."

"Hopefully longer than those little animals," Reggie spat at him. "You did it, too. It wasn't just that monster."

"I had to play along. I always have to play along."

Aaron pulled Reggie away.

"Reggie, forget about the damn rats. He captured Keech. Let's get to work."

Reggie tried to push past the Kassner twin but he blocked her path into the kitchen.

"You need to tell me how you do it. Before you go in there and try to kill that thing, you need to tell me. I have to know."

Aaron stepped in front of Reggie. He looked like a child next to a tree.

"She doesn't have to tell you anything, Mitch. She's here to do a job. And if you stay out of our way, maybe she'll bring back what's left of your brother."

"Will I know him? Will he know me? How are you so sure you won't fail?"

Reggie took the key and stared up at him.

"I won't fail. Now get out of my way."

The boy took a deep breath and moved aside. Reggie walked into the cafeteria and saw the weak yellow light spilling out from the small square near the top of the walk-in freezer door. Ice lined the edges of the window and wisps of smoke circled inside. A padlock dangled from the bar lowered across the door.

She approached and stared into the softly lit freezer.

The body inside looked like a barely animated corpse. He had been stripped down to his underwear, and his skin was a frozen white. He'd been beaten much more severely than his brother, with dark bruises marking his face and torso. Blood had dripped and frozen into crimson crystals beneath his flattened, broken nose. His mouth had been gagged with a bloody strip of shirt. But the monstrous black veins that covered his entire body revealed the thing as an inhuman monster.

She twisted the key inside the lock and popped it open.

"Reggie," Aaron said softly behind her. "Please be careful. If what you find inside —"

"I'll be okay."

Reggie pulled the lock from the bar and lifted the cold handle. The freezer door swung open.

"Get him back, Halloway." The Kassner twin opened the freezer door wide.

Reggie handed Aaron the flashlight and stepped inside. As she walked toward the shivering creature, the thing lifted its eyes and looked at her with a tired and pained panic. It glanced at her and then at Aaron behind her. Its eyes twitched and it shook its head from side to side.

"I'm coming to get you." Reggie was grim and determined.

Aaron looked on, assessing the brute. Those big, burly hands that used to beat on him now hung limply at the Vour's sides, cuts and scars circling his wrists.

Cuts on his wrists.

A jolt of fear burned through Aaron. They were the cuts from the duct tape he had used in the alley. This wasn't Keech — this was *Mitch*.

The Vour had them trapped.

"Get in," it urged behind Aaron. "I think I hear someone coming."

Aaron stood still for a second, and his frosted breath wafted up in front of him. Then with a yell he whipped around and slammed the flashlight into the side of Keech's head. The surprised Vour dropped hard to the ground. Aaron set upon him like a wild animal, the anger boiling up in him giving him a freakish strength. He beat Keech over and over with the flashlight, kicking him in the ribs as he squirmed on the ground and tried to crawl away.

"Nice try, you piece of shit!" Aaron rammed the front of his foot into Keech's face.

"Aaron! What the hell are you doing?" Reggie raced over and grabbed Aaron's arm, but he threw her off.

"You think I give a damn if it was you or the monster you? It makes no difference to me!"

"Aaron! Stop it!"

"It's Keech, Reggie!" He leaned over the Vour, panting and red in the face. "*This one* is Keech."

"Aren't you clever, Cole." Keech coughed up blood and tried to stand, but Aaron crashed the flashlight down on his head one final time, and with a last *crack* Keech lost consciousness.

"Yeah. I'm clever. And you're done, you prick."

Reggie ran back into the freezer and ripped the gag from Mitch's mouth. Up close she could see that the marks had been crudely drawn onto his frozen skin with a black marker.

"Help . . ."

"We'll get you out of here, Mitch. You'll be all right."

"Not me."

The beaten, freezing boy looked into Reggie's face. Crystal tears lined the bottom of his bruised eyes. Then his gaze shifted past her to the twin left bleeding and unconscious on the floor just outside the freezer.

"Help him."

Aaron dragged Keech's unconscious body into the freezer by his ankle. He dropped the leg unceremoniously. Reggie untied Mitch's hands and used the frosty rope to secure Keech's wrists behind him. Then she helped Mitch stand.

"Take him, Aaron. Find him some clothes or a blanket."

"I'll make sure he doesn't die," Aaron answered.

His voice was flat. Reggie caught his hand as he guided Mitch out of the freezer.

"That was some display back there. And you saved me. Now let it go."

He offered her a slight smile and nodded.

"Good hunting," he said. "And be careful." Then he shut the freezer door, and Reggie was alone with the Vour.

15

Reggie knelt beside Keech and patted the side of his bloody cheek with her hand.

"I want you awake for this. Get up."

Keech's eyelids fluttered and opened. He looked up and gasped, the conscious sensation of the deep cold finally registering in him. When he let out a breath, a small puff of black smoke expelled like a coughed-up insect and dispersed into nothing.

"That's right. Your game is over," she said.

The monster inside roiled. Reggie felt its malice.

"No. My game is just beginning."

Reggie moved her hand to Keech's throat and pushed with her mind. She had learned with Henry that to go into the fearscape she needed to be in contact with the Vour's pulse, and now Keech's throbbed against her fingertips. The confines of the freezer warped and undulated. She closed her eyes and started to fall. The descent engulfed her and all went black.

An eternal moment later, she was seated in a giant overstuffed chair. A long space with sharply sloping walls and a low ceiling enclosed her. Furniture stood under white sheets like a crowd of ghosts, illuminated by a single twilit window, and a glass-fronted cabinet towered in the far corner. Piles of junk rose everywhere, and dust stung her nose and throat.

The most outer place of Keech's fearscape was an old attic.

She understood how a place like this would frighten a child, but to her it came as something of a relief.

"I was expecting something a bit more blood and guts."

The Vour had taken him years ago. Keech's essence undoubtedly suffered somewhere much more sinister, lost in a darker realm of fear than this. The dust and stench of decay marked an environment abandoned by the boy's mind; he had long since been lured into worse places. Places she'd soon visit.

But right now, she needed a way down.

She picked up a sheet of paper among a heap of moth-eaten clothes and old curtains. It was a child's crayon drawing of two boys, both in identical red shirts and blue pants, smiling on green grass under a yellow sun. The young artist had signed it with awkward capital letters: *Keech*. The picture was a shred of hope the boy had left behind. She'd found similar symbols inside Henry's fearscape: a treasured stuffed animal, a family photograph.

These small remnants of innocence served as emotional bread crumbs left behind by Vour victims as they spiraled deeper and deeper into the fearscape.

Reggie folded the child's drawing and put it in her pocket.

Floorboards creaked as she stepped over stacks of old magazines and sports equipment. When she moved past a red-eyed rocking horse, it wavered back and forth, then stopped. The toy's face was twisted with agony, and Reggie realized with horror that it wasn't a toy at all, but a real miniature horse whose hooves were nailed to the wooden rockers. It whinnied miserably, and Reggie stuck out her hand to stroke its snout, trying to soothe it. It nuzzled against her, then licked her palm. Reggie screamed and jumped back — the horse's saliva was like acid, and it burned through her skin. She wiped her hand on the chair upholstery, but the damage had been done: half her palm was eaten away. There was no blood, but the hole in her hand emitted a gray smoke.

Reggie focused on the wound and absorbed the intense pain. She'd experienced similarly brutal injuries in Henry's fearscape that had later appeared as faint black scars in the real world. The marks had since faded and left little trace, though Quinn had noticed, but it had proved that harm done to her in the fearscape had dangerous repercussions. From time to time, she had wondered if such wounds could ever truly heal.

But right now now she needed to find a way out of the attic.

In the dim light she saw an outline of a trapdoor in the wooden floor. There was an iron handle with a small keyhole beside it. Reggie looked around for the key, when something shifted in the giant cabinet across the room.

As she drew closer, a score of tiny round heads looked back at her through the cabinet's glass-fronted doors. Rows of white-faced porcelain dolls stared at her with sets of cold blue eyes, their lips all set in unwavering smiles. She peered at them, but none moved.

She knelt down and gripped the trapdoor's metal ring, but no matter how hard she yanked on the door, it wouldn't budge. Something rustled behind her, and she whipped around. The dolls stood in neat rows at attention with their unblinking eyes locked on her.

She glanced around the room, looking for something to use as a lever to pry open the trapdoor. A high-pitched giggle came from the cabinet.

Reggie turned her head slowly and gasped.

Behind the glass, all the dolls stood as they had except for one. A doll with dark curls hung from a noose made of yarn, and she swung faintly back and forth.

Reggie opened the cabinet doors and lifted up the hanged figurine. At that instant the arms of all the other dolls shot up, pointing at Reggie. They opened their mouths in unison and began to shriek. Reggie clamped her hands over her ears as the piercing wail shattered the glass.

The scream was so loud and so high it made Reggie's teeth ache and throb. She could feel warm liquid welling up inside her ears and within moments blood was flowing from them and pouring down the sides of her neck.

Reggie sprang up and snatched one of the dolls from the case. She yanked off its head, and the dead blue eyes rolled back like a shark's, but instead of quelling the scream it swelled into an ocean of hellish noise. Reggie feared the sound would drive her insane. Blood dripped from her nostrils, and her vision clouded over as spurts of red sprang from the pores in her eyes. The pressure building in her head crushed against her skull. Meanwhile, the doll's needlelike fingernails scratched at her forearm. She ripped its arm off and black smoke flooded out from the socket. She dropped the arm to the ground.

The dismembered arm scuttled across the floor, crawling on its porcelain fingers like a crab. Reggie threw the disfigured doll away and snatched up the little hand. It tried to slit her wrist with its nails, but Reggie held it at bay, and stuck one of the fingers into the trapdoor's keyhole. She twisted the doll's hand in the lock and it popped open. The door swung up.

The screaming continued as Reggie looked down into bottomless darkness. She scrambled around the attic, gathering up the sheets and curtains and tying them together. Blood cascaded from her ears and eyes now, and she was nearly blind and deaf. But she frantically worked, praying that she'd stay conscious until she had enough to make an attempt down into the dark. She looped one end to the front leg of the glass cabinet and dropped fifty feet of makeshift rope down through the trapdoor. She wiped her eyes once last time, smearing blood across her hands, and climbed down. Five, ten, twenty feet.

The screams faded as she descended, and Reggie began to gather herself once again. The blood stopped flowing, her ears stopped pounding, and her vision cleared. As she wiped the blood from her face with the sheet, she saw a flickering light above.

Another porcelain doll stood on the edge of the trapdoor, a lit match in its tiny hand. Reggie thought she saw a grin as the thing released the match and set the rope on fire.

Reggie tried to hurry downward, but the flames moved quickly, slipping gleefully down the fabric ladder. Above her, the little doll waved. The fire reached her fingers and Reggie let go, plummeting into the black abyss.

She landed with a bone-crunching thud, sprawled across a gritty floor. A flight of rickety stairs rose over her. Groaning, she sat up, and the surroundings began to take form in the gloom.

She was now in an old-fashioned New England cellar. Cobweb-draped lightbulbs dangled from the rafters, casting a grimy light all around. Moldering walls of stone rose up from a packed dirt floor. The cellar stretched on into the shadows, and the stairs led up into an inscrutable darkness.

An elderly woman's voice screeched from above, "Naughty children stay down in the dark place! You'll be here until you've learned your lesson!"

A dead bolt clacked into place, echoing down the steps. Reggie wondered what the lesson was. She stood up.

The place was a dungeon. Beads of water dripped down the walls and gathered in rank pools. Reggie's stomach fluttered at the sight of little red spiders scurrying in the cobwebs overhead. Melted plastic soldiers, broken cars, and gutted teddy bears covered the floor. These were the boys' first victims.

Reggie stepped over them and tried the stairs, but the first step turned to dust under her foot. Soon the entire staircase crumbled before her eyes. There had to be another way out — an escape other than an unseen door at the top of a disintegrating staircase.

She searched for clues to understand this fearscape. Mason jars crowded a few dilapidated shelves. She plucked up one of them and wiped away the dust, preparing herself for whatever horror might be inside. Much to her surprise, she saw it contained bright orange peaches. After blowing the dust from a few more jars, she found a variety of tasty-looking fruits and vegetables and tried to twist open a jar, but the lid was sealed too tight.

Keech must have been kept down here for long stretches of time without any food. As a small child, he would have been able to reach the jars, but not strong enough to open them. And smashing them open probably prompted a severe beating.

She hurled the jar against the wall. Glass shards flew back at her like shrapnel and she ducked. The fruit splattered against the stone, bursting like organs.

A gory stain oozed down the wall.

A cat's low meow came from the dark shadows of the cellar. Another replied. The heated panting of a dog joined the chorus, along with several croaking frogs. Scores of animal eyes, like tiny yellow mirrors, glinted though the darkness at Reggie. Their paws and flippers, their snake-bellies and insect wings, brought them into the grimy light. These were the twins' other — later — victims. Limping, squirming, and dragging, the casualties of the young Kassners' terrible acts drew closer.

A skinned cat crept out from the shadows, its vertebrae like long white caterpillars tied together with oily thread. A puppy with only a lower jaw blindly stumbled after, the top of its head pulped like a melon beneath a hammer. Its tongue dangled from its roots over the side of broken teeth. A burned raccoon peered out through wet, empty sockets from behind a broken barrel. Frogs and toads with torched skin, wingless moths, bisected worms, and other tortured things writhed toward her.

Reggie wondered if the Vours appreciated the irony. They enjoyed such brutality, but the Kassner boys must have committed these atrocities *before* one of them fell victim to a Vour. Keech had lashed out against innocent animals because he'd been tortured himself as a child, and now his victims had come back to haunt him in his fearscape.

"Poor creatures," Reggie murmured.

The flayed cat hissed. All of the animals' eyes burned with hate. It wasn't pity they were after.

It was revenge.

Reggie backed away, desperately searching for a way out.

A dime-size speck shone to her right in the gore stain on the wall. It was a hole, and light came through the other side. The animals dragged themselves closer. Reggie balled her hand into a fist and punched the wall as hard as she could.

Her fist landed solidly on the small hole. Pain reverberated up her arm and shoulder, but a large crack formed from floor to ceiling. The tide of crippled bugs and mangled frogs boiled at her feet. The skinless cat crouched to pounce.

Reggie stepped back from the crack, took a breath, and charged the wall with her shoulder. It gave way with the roar of an earthquake just as the cat leapt through the air, its skin trailing behind it, its bloody claws barely missing her. She charged through the dusty rubble and burst into the bright light.

When she looked behind her, Reggie found none of the nightmare creatures. In fact, there was no trace of the cellar at all. A bright gold savannah stretched out to the horizon. Beautiful but barren, it looked like the sort of landscape she'd seen in

Animal Planet documentaries about Africa. This was a far more desolate version, though. No trees offered shade, no bugs whirred and buzzed, no birds flew or chattered.

Reggie surveyed the vast scrubby nothingness spreading out in all directions. The sun blazed directly overhead. It was a lonely and hostile place, without direction or comfort.

This must be how the young Keech saw the world.

The relentless sun beat down on her. Her mouth grew dry, her feet throbbed, and the acid from the horse's tongue had eaten deeper into her palm; she held up her hand to shade her eyes, and light poured through a thin membrane of skin.

The cellar had been cold and damp, and she immediately longed for that darkness. The heat was torturous and she could do nothing but move forward.

And that was precisely what the Vour wanted, exactly how the fearscape had been designed. Once the victim was trapped inside, he would have no choice but to let fear and pain drive him deeper and deeper into the nightmarish prison.

In the distance, a pair of brown rock outcroppings jutted from the plain. They offered no shadow from the harsh and unmoving sun, but they were a change in the landscape. Reggie trudged toward the massive towers, and as she approached, she realized they were identical. They stood like twin stone giants. She passed between them, looking up for any dangers that might lurk overhead, but she saw nothing save the blinding sun.

Her throat burned with thirst, and the first strains of panic stirred inside of her. She could combat dolls and animals. They had scope and size that she could fathom. But how could she fight an enemy like desolation?

There was no escape from the sun, and no visible end to the desert in Keech's mind. All Reggie could do was put one foot in front of the other. She pulled the crayon drawing from her pocket with her wounded hand. The lone ember of hope in this forsaken place gave her little reassurance now.

Though Henry's fearscape had been terrifying and dangerous, the tokens of hope in his nightmare world felt immediate, guideposts leading to a frightened soul that had moved deeper into the fearscape only hours before she'd arrived. But Keech had been gone for years, and as far as Reggie knew, he'd lost his way in the desert of his fears long, long ago.

The rock towers faded into the distance behind her, but nothing appeared on the horizon. Sand, sun, empty sky.

Scalding. Hopeless. Terribly, horribly alone.

Reggie quickly grew delirious from heat and dehydration. It no longer mattered what was real and what was nightmare; her body was reacting to the experiences of her mind — and her mind was dying.

She held her wounded hand up again. The acid had burned all the way through, leaving a quarter-sized cavity in her raw flesh. Reggie could do nothing but try to ignore the throbbing pain, and tell herself over and over that this wasn't real. She peered through the hole in her hand and saw something different now. The change in landscape was subtle, but after the eternity of broiling sameness, it gave her hope.

Black buzzards circled high above a rocky hill topped with

two dead trees. Reggie stumbled forward, tripping over the crags as she climbed. When at last she crested the mound, the stink of what had drawn the buzzards nearly knocked her over.

The valley below teemed with carcasses: lions, rhinos, elephants, and scores of others. They lay in unmoving heaps, picked at by vultures. A putrid wind blew in her face, stirring the blankets of flies that covered the dead. She looked around for what might have killed these beasts, but saw no movement in the bright noon light. Warily she descended.

Some of the bodies had bloated in the heat like balloons, while others rippled with maggots. As Reggie made her way around the decaying animals, she noticed all had one thing in common. They lay in matched pairs and seemed to have died in the throes of battle. They were twins.

She passed a disemboweled leopard, rotted with its jaws clamped on another leopard's throat. Two wildebeests lay unblinking beside one another, their bodies torn and their tusks bloody. Even a pair of snakes rested in a tangled pile.

Examine the pattern, Reggie told herself. Solve the puzzle and find Keech. Was there a rivalry between the siblings? Was one afraid he'd destroy the other? The dead twin animals were a mystery that eluded her. The unmoving sun baked their corpses, and Reggie's tongue swelled with thirst. Flies buzzed around her as she weaved among the bodies.

A glistening up ahead caught her attention.

Giant palm trees swayed over bright blue water, and tall green reeds rustled on its shore. She staggered through the sand toward the oasis, and a cool breeze blew across its water. Reggie collapsed on her knees in the shallows, cupped her hands, and drank. Water leaked through her burnt hand, but she lapped up enough to quell the hot ache in her throat.

The palm trees swayed above, and the reeds rustled. She cleaned the wound on her leg with the clear water. Reggie had no idea what this place could be.

She guessed the life-giving pool had drawn the animals into the valley. But why they came in pairs, and then killed one another, she couldn't understand. This oasis was peaceful.

Reggie looked down into the still pool and saw her reflection. Her dark, sweaty hair formed a tangled halo around her head, and the desert sun had burned her skin a deep mauve.

She bent down and splashed water in her face, then jerked back. Her reflection did not move in synch with her. Instead it continued to stare up at her, serious and still. Reggie turned her head to one side, then the other, but her mirror image remained transfixed.

Suddenly, the figure burst from the water's surface and grabbed her by the throat. Reggie fell backward, the face she'd always seen in the mirror now leering and hideous. The copy tightened its hands around Reggie's neck. She lashed out and hit her double under the chin. Bright light flashed in Reggie's eyes, and pain exploded in her own jaw.

The hands released her throat. They both scrambled to their feet.

Reggie and her double circled. Every detail was replicated: her fresh sunburn, her disfigured palm, the doll scratches on her arms — all of it. Her evil twin glared back, eyes wild and bloodshot, mouth fixed in a snarl. A bruise was forming on its chin where Reggie had struck it. Reggie felt the ache on her own face as well.

"What do you want?" Reggie asked.

The double lashed out and clawed at Reggie's face. She backed away, but not quickly enough. The nails scraped down her cheek to her chin. Reggie felt hot pain, and saw the bright red scratches reflected on the double's cheek.

Her eyes flitted left and right, trying to find an escape route. There was none, only the water, or the valley where all the others had died. A rock slightly bigger than her fist lay by the waterside a few feet away. She snatched it up and raised it like a hammer. The doppelgänger crouched defensively, anticipating the attack.

Reggie didn't want to kill her twin, but it seemed to be the rules of this place. Survival of the fittest. Reggie dove at the double, and the two rolled a few feet, scratching and clawing and biting at each other. Reggie ignored the sting of the wounds, and wrestled the double to the ground, pinning her down with her knees. It glared up at her, its eyes solid with fury, but said nothing. Reggie held the rock above her, preparing to bring it down hard on her attacker's head.

Then she thought of the dead beasts in the desert, the scrapes on the double's cheek, and the pain in her own jaw. What injuries one inflicted on the other, they both received. If Reggie smashed its skull, she would most likely bash out her own brains, too.

The antagonism between the twins destroyed them both. Was that the root of Keech's fears?

Think, Reggie told herself. Rivalry. These deaths were about rivalries. She didn't know what Keech and Mitch's relationship had been when they were boys, but here each twin was angry and wanted to defeat the other. And here that was impossible because of an invisible link between them. Hurting one hurt the other.

She didn't need to overpower her double — she couldn't. They needed to be equals — sisters, not enemies.

Reggie threw the stone into the pool and held up her hands.

The double howled and seized Reggie by the throat again. But Reggie did not fight; instead she reached out and put her arms around her. The twin's hands tightened on her neck, but Reggie didn't flinch.

"Stop."

The hands loosened. Reggie gently pulled the double closer to her and embraced her. Her twin tensed, then relaxed. It smiled once before dissipating like mist on a cool wind.

Reggie touched her cheek. The scrape closed under her fingertips, though she could still feel the trace of a scar.

She looked down and saw a green crayon sticking out of the sand, the wax miraculously unmelted in the heat. A second breadcrumb. She was getting closer.

Reggie picked up the crayon and put it with the drawing.

She heard a roar, and the lake began to rotate in a receding whirlpool, like the plug had been pulled from a giant bathtub. Soon, a field of wet silt was all that remained of the clear blue waters.

Reggie walked out into the drained oasis. There, in its center, was a perfectly circular metal grate. She pulled it open like a hatch to reveal a round, concrete passage that plunged straight down. Iron rungs protruded from the wall, still dripping with water. Reggie climbed down into the dark, and the ladder's passage opened up into a large cavern.

She dropped from the last rung onto a stone ledge, and in the center of the cave was a giant rusty cage, big enough to hold a delivery truck.

Flickering torches on the wall cast light across the giant thing that slept inside. Creeping closer, circling around the corroded bars, she took a long look at the prisoner.

It was humanoid, sleeping on its side with a hand over its face. From the way it was huddled inside the cell, Reggie guessed it would stand over ten feet tall, with blobby arms and legs that looked swollen and tumescent. Reggie thought if she stuck a pin in the creature it might rupture. It looked like a Kassner, or at least like a demonic form of one with sharp, exaggerated facial features and skin specked with black. The thing's breaths came deep and even, and now and then it snored.

The monster stirred as she circled around the cage.

A distended and rumpled wad of flesh grew from the thing's broad back. Two spindly arms protruded from the lump, twitching and jerking, and a misshapen head with eyes that appeared sealed behind seamless eyelids.

Reggie stared in revulsion, puzzling over the pitiful abomination.

Who is Keech and who is Mitch?

Only one way to find out.

"Keech," she whispered.

The lump's fleshy lids opened, and its gray, watery eyes widened in terror. Reggie squeezed through the bars and tiptoed toward it.

"Keech," she said. "It's okay. We're going to leave this place."

The tiny mouth was a crude hole that trembled with a wet slurping sound.

"No. Can't leave without the big one."

She reached up and touched his emaciated hand.

"You don't need Mitch to survive, Keech."

"Mitch . . ."

"You're strong, Keech. And part of you is still good."

The eyes blinked, and its lower lip quivered. "Bad. That's why we're locked in the dark place."

"Good kids can do bad things," she said. "But they can make up for it." Reggie reached into her back pocket and pulled out the folded-up piece of paper, the cheerful crayon drawing she'd found in the attic. She held it up to Keech and smiled. "Is this yours?"

The head nodded and stammered, "I like to draw."

"Would you draw something for me?"

"I lost all my crayons."

"I found one." Reggie held out the green crayon and the lump looked with wonder at it. It took it in its nubby fingers and held it, then it began to color the air with it. Reggie marveled at the green swirls that appeared out of nowhere. They were faint at first, then grew in vibrancy. With every stroke of the crayon, the figure looked more boyish, until only the thinnest graft of skin tethered it to the ugly monster. The boy looked a bit older than

Henry, and he wore a red baseball jersey and blue jeans. Reggie took his hands.

And then the hulking beast awoke.

Mitch.

The monster thrashed awake and twisted to face the intruder. Bones creaked and cartilage snapped. The beast howled in agony and fury. It lunged at Reggie, but she dove and tumbled away, scrambling in the dirt to the opposite side of the cage. The right arm of the behemoth lodged between two rusty bars of its prison, and it struggled to pull itself free.

"You woke the bad me," said the boy. "Go. Go before I hurt you like I hurt everything."

"Talk to Mitch! Tell him to stop!"

"Mitch isn't here. Just me. Only me." The boy was terrified. "I lost him a long time ago. I'm all alone here."

And then Reggie understood.

The doppelgänger in the pond, the identical beasts locked in deathblows, the vast and empty desert. This fearscape wasn't about being a weaker sibling. Keech's deepest fear wasn't of his brother.

Most of all, he feared himself.

As a young boy his personality had split, the dark half opening a black maw inside him to swallow pain and anger while the light half withered like rotten fruit. And in this place, all that was good in the boy had been consumed.

"You're not alone anymore," Reggie said. "And you're coming with me."

Reggie took the boy's hands again and heaved backward.

Flesh ripped and the skin holding beast and boy together tore apart. The monster roared in agony.

"Come on!"

Reggie and Keech slipped through the bars as a massive fist slammed against the cage, rocking it back and forth.

Keech stood paralyzed with fear as his monstrous self rattled the bars and bellowed. The roars echoed throughout the cave, shaking every stone. Boulders tumbled down the walls, and stalactites plummeted like daggers into the floor. The monster bent the bars of the cage and forced itself through the widened opening. Keech just crouched on the ground, huddled into a little ball.

Reggie kneeled beside him. "Remember your drawings?" Her voice was thin like a breeze. "Draw a picture for us."

Keech gazed at the crayon in his hand. He held it up to her.

"Here. You do it."

The monster was free now and almost upon them. Reggie did not look up at it.

"I can't." She smiled gently at him. "I can't do it for you. Draw what you want to see happen."

The boy held up the crayon and drew a green lasso in the air. It looped around the monster's head, and Keech cinched it tight. The creature gasped and lost its balance. It fell over and landed with a crack, and smoke began to seep out its nostrils. It writhed violently on the ground, its furious convulsions pulling down the walls of the cave around them. Reggie searched frantically for another exit, but there was none.

"Keech. Get us out of here."

He thought for a moment, and the monster wrenched the lasso off its head. It threw it to the side and held a claw out toward its weaker half. The boy wavered and reached back, dropping the crayon in the dirt, but Reggie caught his hand.

"You can do this!" She grabbed up the crayon and wrapped his fingers around it. Keech nodded.

He drew a rectangle in the air, then a circle in the middle of it. He grasped the circle and turned it; the knob twisted, and the door out of this hell swung open, revealing a light on the other side. The monster howled and ran at them. Reggie started through the door, but Keech hesitated.

"What's over there?" he asked.

She grasped his hand.

"Mitch."

Hand-in-hand, the two stepped into the light as the cavern collapsed, and the rest of the fearscape fell away into nothingness.

16

Reggie returned to a groggy consciousness on the floor of the freezer, her head pressed to Keech's chest. For a moment her exhausted mind told her she was seven or eight years old and waking up after a nap on the couch in front of the television — a little child who'd fallen asleep on her dad.

But the piercing cold and rasping wheeze coming from Keech's lungs made her sit up. The moist and frigid air spun in a frenzied cyclone over her head, but the vapor was no longer a wispy white. It had turned noxious and inky black.

The expelled monster whipped around the dim pale bulb that dangled from the ceiling, a terrible and wicked thing desperately hunting for heat. The entity looked like a repulsive comet with an oily tail, and at the head, a disturbing blob morphed and convulsed.

Reggie could make out the mimicked face of a young Keech in between the erratic pulsations, as if the Vour fought to retain the innocent boy it had consumed years ago. But it could not hold the human features; the face sagged and dispersed into amoebic rings. The Vour clung to the edge of existence, and watching it panic in its last throes did not give Reggie the satisfaction she'd anticipated.

In a final thrust of anger, the unstable monster surged and smashed against Reggie's face. The putrid mist broke all around her head, and she smelled the Vour's fear of death as plainly as the blunt scent of fresh road kill. She thought of Eben, and she closed her eyes and tried to hold her breath, refusing to inhale the poison.

"*Ours . . .*"

The thing spoke like untilled dirt. It had come apart and hung in the cold air for a torturous moment more. The voice emanated from nowhere and everywhere, and Reggie heard an ancient chorus of evil things echo in her mind.

"*You will be ours . . .*"

And then it was gone. A residue of sickly moisture clung to Reggie's bare skin, but the monster was no more.

Keech coughed, shallow and weak at first, then louder, stronger, as cold air flushed his lungs and the oxygen rushed into his brain, a mind no longer bound and corrupted.

"Keech . . ."

Mitch, wrapped in white towels from the school gym, had opened the freezer door and stumbled inside, his eyes circled with deep black bruises caused by the harsh break in his nose.

Aaron walked inside a few paces behind him, sullen and silent. He looked immediately to Reggie and nodded.

Mitch knelt down next to his stirring brother.

"Keech? It's me. Can you hear me?"

Keech's eyelids opened slowly like those of a newborn. He

squinted and blinked repeatedly. He licked his cut lip and swallowed, parched and sore. He touched his brother's cheek.

"I know you."

He sounded surprised by the sound of his own deep voice.

Mitch placed a calloused but gentle hand beneath his brother's head and helped him sit up. And then he lifted Keech to his feet, absorbing all of his weak sibling's weight.

Mitch turned to Reggie as Keech sagged against his shoulder.

"Thanks. I owe you."

The twins walked out of the freezer and into the dark cafeteria. There would be more police tomorrow. School, though over for the summer, would be shut down and cordoned off. Questions. Media. Another investigation.

But that would be tomorrow.

Now the feeling came back, along with the pain from the wounds she'd received in the fearscape. Her hands, in particular, ached. She examined her palm where the acid had burned her; grayish scar tissue marred her skin, and when she pressed it black smoke seeped out. In a twisted way it was like popping a blister. Aaron took Reggie's hand and examined it.

"Does it hurt?"

"No."

"Reggie. I'm worried about this. With what happened to Eben. The coughing and —"

"Not now, Aaron. Please?"

He nodded and draped a towel across her shoulders. They exited the freezer, and he held her as they moved slowly down the hallway.

A silhouette appeard down the dimly lit corridor.

"Finals are over, you two. Congratulations, you both passed. And you, Reggie, earned an A for your extra credit work tonight."

Mr. Machen flicked on the hallway lights. He held a handgun loosely at his side.

"What the hell?" Aaron shielded Reggie.

"Oh, God, Aaron. He's one of them." Reggie's mind was fatigued beyond human capacity, and the shocking appearance of Machen was more than she could bear. "In class — the one who gave me the vision — he's a *Vour*."

Aaron ran at Machen before he could raise the weapon. But the English teacher merely snatched hold of Aaron's wrist and turned, flipping the boy across the floor using his own momentum against him. Then he scratched his temple with the gun and shook his head in disappointment.

"Please give me a little more credit. Would I really expose myself as a Vour after what you just did in that freezer?"

"Then who are you? A cop?"

"No, no. I operate outside of certain laws. Not much unlike another of your acquaintances."

"Wait, you're a Tracer?"

"Is anyone in this town who they say they are?" Aaron stood up and rubbed his wrist. "Is it something in the water or what?"

"We have a lot to talk about," Machen continued. "But not here. Broken entry, butchered animals. Not very subtle. Follow me."

"Why would we follow you?" Reggie asked.

Machen was already walking briskly toward the gymnasium. He wagged his gun in the air but did not turn around.

Aaron looked at Reggie. "He may have information about the solstice, Reg. We should hear him out."

"Well I guess it's a good thing I told my dad I was spending the night at your place."

Aaron took Reggie's hand again and pulled her down the hallway. Machen held open the door at the gym exit.

"Hurry. The police are out front arresting the Kassners."

Reggie's heart sank. So much for a brotherly reunion.

They slinked through the parking lot toward the woods behind the school. Blue and red lights pulsed against the high branches and leaves, but Reggie tried to put the Kassners out of her mind. There was nothing to be done now.

Once clear of the school grounds, Machen turned on the flashlight Aaron had left behind and guided the two teens deep into the grove. He had set up a small camp with a one-man tent amid the deep brush, an inconspicuous hideout he'd used to keep an eye on the school.

"How did you know we'd come here?" Aaron asked.

"Your phone, Aaron. It's tapped. Easier to tap cell phones than wires. Just ride the signal."

"Like I'm not paranoid enough already."

Reggie stalked over to Machen.

"So I'm here. Tell me what you can do to help, or pack up your crap house and get the hell out. I don't care what sort of secret anti-boogeyman organization you belong to — give me something

I can use to destroy these things, or I'll call the cops myself and tell them there's a pervert hiding out in the woods, spying on underage girls in cheering camp."

Machen laughed.

"You don't understand, Reggie. The Tracers thought they knew everything they needed to know. People turn into Vours, we find them and eradicate them. Clean and simple. Our fraternity has been doing it for centuries. But now you've turned the whole thing upside down. Cutter's Wedge's very own Puck."

"What do you mean I've turned it all upside down?" Reggie asked. "I brought my brother back. And I saved Keech Kassner."

"And your kind would have murdered them," Aaron added.

"Not murder. Extermination."

"Your way is no longer acceptable." Reggie looked Machen straight in the eye. "No more murder."

"I do what's necessary."

"Not anymore. I —"

"This isn't just about *you*, Reggie. These monsters have destroyed lives, communities — entire civilizations. You have no idea what you are dealing with here."

"Who did you lose?" Reggie asked.

"I'm not here to —"

"A brother? A sister? Tell me."

Machen stood silent. And when he finally spoke, it was without emotion. Like he'd moved beyond feeling.

"My wife. My sons. When the Vours found out that I had discovered their existence, they murdered everyone I loved."

"I'm sorry."

Machen paced, twigs snapping below his boots. "Did Eben tell you that he was discharged from the Tracers?"

"No. I didn't even know you guys existed until a few hours ago," said Reggie.

"Well, he was," said Machen. "After he failed to kill your brother."

"What?" Aaron gasped.

Reggie said nothing.

"His job was to eliminate Vours. He should have taken out Henry, but he didn't, so he was sacked. They sent me as his replacement. Not to kill Henry," Machen added hastily. "It appears your brother is recovered. But in addition to taking care of any threats, my orders were to observe you and find out more about this power of yours. But the Vours lay low for six months, so I had nothing. Not until last Friday, anyway."

"So you knew what was happening in class," said Reggie.

"What's the point of telling us now?" Aaron asked.

"I saw something I never expected to see," said Machen. "A Vourized human brought back. A Vour destroyed. We should be working together, Reggie, don't you see? We can help each other."

"How's that?"

"The Tracers have an extensive network. Lots of resources. And you have a singular perspective on how the Vours operate. Maybe, working together, we can defeat them for good."

Aaron pursed his lips and shrugged. "What do you know about the Vours and the summer solstice?" he asked.

Machen considered the question.

"Almost nothing. The Vours are usually quieter at the solstice — their hallucinatory powers are weaker this time of year, though no one knows why. But they have been more active this summer."

"Keen observation," Reggie said dryly.

"We've had evidence suggesting the Vours are planning something big on the solstice," Aaron said. "Think your 'resources' could look into it?"

"I'll see what I can find out. In the meantime, keep quiet. No more breaking into buildings. I can't help you if you get locked up. As far as this town knows, I'm just an English teacher." He handed Aaron his flashlight. "One question for you, Reggie. Your vision in class. What did you see?"

"I saw my brother as a killer. My deepest fear."

"Be careful, Reggie," Machen said. "I doubt you know what your deepest fear really is. Your mind won't let you. But these monsters will try and find it. Don't let them."

17

Reggie was so sore and tired she didn't want to get out of bed Sunday morning. Machen had driven around for an hour before dropping them off, quizzing Reggie on everything she knew about the Vours, how she'd gotten her abilities, what fearscapes were like, and tons of other questions, many of which Reggie had no clue about. He promised to report back to the Tracers and find out what he could about a Vour solstice plot.

At noon Reggie went back to the hospital to see Eben, as she'd promised she would, but the doctors had put him on meds to make him sleep.

"He had an epileptic fit this morning," the nurse explained.

"Is he going to be okay?" Reggie asked.

"I can't say, dear. But I'll tell him you were here."

That afternoon, Reggie picked up the phone at least a half dozen times with the intent to call Aaron and tell him about Quinn. Keech was saved now; Aaron seemed to be recovering from his ordeal in prison. She shouldn't keep such a secret from her best friend, her confidant, her partner in all this madness. But each time, she put the phone back into its cradle without dialing.

What would she say to him? That she had already teamed up with the monster that had tried to kill him out on the lake, and could he suck it up and fall in line, thanks very much?

There was something else. Reggie knew that Aaron would feel horribly betrayed, and rightfully so. He had always stood by her no matter what, and now she was deliberately keeping him in the dark. She sensed the threads of her life spiraling out of control, and guilt churned within her. She hadn't meant for it to go this far. The anger, hurt, and jealousy Aaron would feel when he found out — would he forgive her for what she'd done? Would he lose sight of the big picture and go after Quinn? Start down a path that would undoubtedly lead to one of them ending up dead?

"Are you actually going to call someone, or are you just doing random checks for a dial tone?" Dad asked, walking into the family room. "I paid the phone bill this month, I promise."

Reggie looked up, startled. She smiled weakly and stood up.

"Oh, no, I was just thinking."

"What about?"

"Just stuff."

Dad nodded grimly. "Not about disappearing Tuesday morning before we go to Thornwood, I hope."

"No, definitely not thinking about that. I'll be here, Dad."

"Good. I think you'll get a lot out of it, Reg. Dr. Unger is a good guy."

Or a sadistic fear monster, Reggie thought.

Dad approached her curiously.

"What is that?" he asked. "You have a mark on your face."

Reggie's hand flew to her cheek. She'd forgotten all about the scar from the fearscape.

"And your hand — and your arms! Reggie, where did these bruises come from?"

"Oh, I — I fell. Off my bike. The roads were slick on my way back from the hospital — no biggie."

"Okay." Dad looked doubtful. "You know I'd want you to tell me if something was really wrong. No matter what it is."

"I know," Reggie replied.

Monday was Aaron's day off, so they spent the time researching the amygdala theory. Reggie had told him it was something she had been thinking about after studying for their biology final.

"Ha. I knew you were shitting me on that whole 'I don't do science' thing. This is genius!" Aaron leaped at the concept that Vours entered humans through their brains, as Reggie guessed he would, but by nightfall they had come up with nothing of particular use.

Tuesday morning dawned sunny and humid, like the days before it. The drive to Thornwood was lined with pear trees in full bloom, leafy explosions of white petals against the backdrop of green horse pastures. Reggie, Dad, and Henry had not spoken since they'd all piled into the truck.

Reggie expected a cheerless, clinical structure, all white walls and steel. So when they rounded the final bend in the road she was startled to see a beautiful white manor house surrounded by well-tended gardens and lawns. Other outbuildings, including a barn and stables, were scattered over the property. It all looked much more like a country inn than a psychiatric institution, and the idyllic setting only made Reggie that much more uneasy.

Dad parked the truck, and Henry hopped out to lead the way through the front door into the lobby. They were asked to wait in a cozy den with overstuffed armchairs, candle sconces on the walls, and a fireplace. And when the nurse led them to Dr. Unger's office, it was not down white, sterilized corridors, but rather a wood-paneled hall decorated with black and white photographs of local historical buildings. Reggie realized that, far from being a cold and sterile environment, Thornwood seemed like a comfortable and pleasant home, certainly not a bastion of demonic mad scientists.

Dr. Unger sat behind a large oak desk in his office, an open and light-filled study lined with bookshelves and more photographs; toys, art supplies, and children's furniture were in one corner of the room. Reggie had seen him the previous week when he had come to the elementary school, but she had not yet officially met him. He was an older man, with a mane of white hair and wire glasses through which peered twinkling blue eyes. He had ruddy cheeks and a hooked nose, and he stooped a little when he walked. He looked a bit like Santa in a white lab coat instead of red fur.

He rose immediately as the Halloways entered and approached them warmly.

"Thom, excellent. I'm so glad we could work this out. Good to see you again, Henry. And you must be Reggie." He held out his hand toward her. "Charles Unger."

"Hello." Reggie took his hand and shook it. She wondered, if he was a Vour, if she would feel something when she touched him, if there would be some sign, some spark, that would betray him. But she only felt an old man's wrinkled and arthritic hand, only saw his kind eyes smiling at her, welcoming her.

"Please, let's all sit down," he said, gesturing to the child-sized chairs.

For the next hour, Unger facilitated a family session, and Reggie tried to answer his questions like a normal teen girl might. *No*, she wasn't resentful of her father, but *yes*, she felt like he was out of touch with her needs. *Yes*, she was angry with her mother and *maybe* she transferred those emotions into bad behavior with her father and brother.

All in all it was normal shrink stuff, but Reggie remained anxious; her mind darted to the possible horrors that were going on unseen in this facility.

Finally Unger gently wrapped up their conversation and politely asked to have ten minutes alone with Dad.

"And Reggie, I hope you found this session helpful. I think we'll make excellent progress together."

"Yes, I do, too."

Reggie shook Unger's hand, and she and Henry left the office. Unger shut the door behind them, leaving them out in the hallway.

"Okay, Hen. Did you feel anything?"

Henry shook his head.

"No, nothing. I don't think Dr. Unger is a Vour, Reg."

"You sure?"

"I . . . I think so."

Reggie walked in the opposite direction of the waiting lounge.

"Let's check out the rest of this place."

They passed several closed doors, and Reggie had Henry stand close to each one, but he never felt the sensation he had the night Quinn was in their house.

"What if someone catches us?"

"We say we got lost."

The hall opened into an atrium, then led up a windy staircase. They found more offices on the second floor.

"Anything?" Reggie asked hopefully.

Henry shook his head.

"I just feel normal."

Reggie sighed and looked at her watch.

"Dad's probably wondering where we are."

"I'm sorry, Reggie."

Reggie put her arm around her brother.

"It's not your fault. I guess I was wrong about this place."

She smiled at Henry as they went back downstairs because she didn't want him to worry, but all she could think of were the four and a half days remaining before the solstice. If Thornwood was not the Vour headquarters, then where was it?

By the time they got out to the car, thunderstorms had started again like so many of the previous days. Thornwood was in a low-lying area, and the driveway was almost completely washed out in the flash flood.

"Looks like there's a maintenance road that leads out the back through the woods," said Dad. "The truck shouldn't have any trouble."

They all packed in the truck and cut over to the access road. It wound through the dense woods, and the pattering of the raindrops on the windows lulled Reggie to sleep.

Suddenly Henry reached out from the backseat and clutched her shoulder. She awoke and turned around.

"I feel it," he said, wide-eyed. "I feel chills."

"I'll turn off the air, bud," Dad said, reaching for the temperature control.

Reggie nodded at Henry and tried to gauge their location. But they were in the middle of the woods, not near anything. Thornwood was at least a mile back. It was wilderness, but Reggie felt a twinge of terrible excitement.

The Vours were out there.

And she was getting closer.

Aaron felt helpless.

He had been studying Web sites for hours, as well as the occult books he had ordered, but nothing seemed helpful in his quest to learn more about Vours. Reggie was at Thornwood, and even though she had promised not to do anything rash, he was on edge. He had to do something, had to find something that would help them know what to do. There was only one other place he could think of that might provide the answers he needed, but it meant betraying a friend's trust.

Aaron slipped on his tennis shoes and dashed down the stairs, rolled his ten-speed out of the garage, and minutes later was coasting out of his neighborhood toward town.

Downtown Cutter's Wedge felt like a ghost town on the stifling summer afternoon after the torrential rain. Aaron noticed steam mirages on the asphalt as he pedaled up in front of Something Wicked and unlocked the door. He stashed his bike in the back room, then opened the cabinet where Eben kept all the store's tax records and invoices. On the bottom shelf was a small safe.

He had watched Eben open the safe many times, mostly to replace the petty cash the storekeeper kept there, and he was fairly certain of the combination. He wasn't sure if Eben was aware he knew it; he himself had never supposed he'd conspire to open it. It took him a few tries, shifting the numbers one spot to the right or left, but eventually the lock clicked, and the safe door swung open.

He removed the pouch of petty cash and receipts and set it aside. The safe's contents included an antique watch that Aaron knew had belonged to Eben's father, a set of house keys, and a single worn file folder.

Aaron took out the keys, put the cash envelope back, and shut the safe door. With keys in hand, he walked up the steep flight of stairs in the back of the store that led to Eben's apartment.

Aaron took the steps slowly, fingering the silver keychain. He unlocked the deadbolt and the knob and opened the door. Its squeaky hinges were the apartment's only alarm.

He looked around Eben's shabby but neat home. It smelled of old leather and used books, much like the shop below. Aaron had been here many times, but always as a guest when his boss was present. He knew Eben's study was at the back of the apartment, so he went there first. He wasn't exactly sure what he was looking for, but he was hoping that in his years as a Vour hunter, Eben had collected information that might help them now.

Next to Eben's desk and computer were rows of file cabinets. Aaron opened the first one; it was filled with manila file folders labeled alphabetically. Aaron pulled out one at the front of the cabinet, marked "Abel, Hiram," and stamped "Closed Case." He flipped through it.

It was a dossier of sorts on this man Hiram Abel, documenting his life from age eight through forty-five. There were photographs, school reports from elementary through college, house titles, employment records from various traveling sales agencies, and several newspaper clippings with his name highlighted.

Aaron skimmed the papers from all across the country; they were primarily reports of tragic suicides. In one a mother of four had drowned herself in a lake, in another a teenage boy had hanged himself from the high school flagpole. In every one, Hiram Abel had been interviewed as a witness, sometimes as a friend, sometimes as a neighbor, sometimes just as a passerby. The last article was from the Macon, Georgia *Gazette*, and it reported that a woman named Alma Abel had carved out her eyes with a steak knife and bled to death on her kitchen floor. She had been discovered by her nine-year-old son, Hiram. The article was dated March 5, 1883.

Aaron grimaced; Abel must have been Vourized when he was a boy, and his first act had been to drive his mother to mutilation. The monster had gotten such a taste for it that he'd spent his adult life traveling the country, mentally terrorizing strangers until they'd killed themselves. This could have been the outcome if Reggie had not destroyed the Vour inside Henry.

The latest article was from 1919, a blurb in a Pittsburgh newspaper reporting the disappearance of Hiram Abel and requesting anyone with knowledge of the incident to notify police. There was no information in the file dated after that, and Aaron guessed why. Abel had been one of Eben's marks, and the Tracer had tracked him and killed him in 1919.

But Eben had said he'd joined the Tracers when he was a teenager. Aaron did some quick calculations in his head: even if Eben had been only fifteen when he had killed Abel, that would make him over a hundred years old today.

"You don't keep small secrets, do you, Eb?" Aaron muttered to himself as he replaced the file and perused another.

All of them contained details on various men and women throughout the previous century; some were marked with the "Closed Case" stamp and some weren't. But from what Aaron could tell, Eben had indeed "liberated" hundreds of souls during his time as a Tracer.

There was nothing, however, that could help Reggie and Aaron now. The files were more like criminal records than exhaustive research about the monsters, and nowhere could Aaron find anything about the solstices or a greater Vour collective. He closed the drawers and glanced around the rest of the room, satisfied that there was nothing else to find here.

He next went to Eben's bedroom. He had not been in here before, and the room was Spartan, with only a twin bed with a threadbare quilt, and a night table with a collection of twentieth century poetry on it. Aaron checked under the bed but found only Eben's leather slippers. A door on the far side of the room led to a small walk-in closet where Eben's tweed jackets and pressed trousers hung. Aaron was about to leave this room as well when he noticed a trunk shoved under the clothes.

He heaved the trunk out into the bedroom. It was a heavy wood, and Aaron broke a sweat even though it was just a few feet. There was a latch on the top, but it was unlocked, and Aaron swung the lid open.

The trunk was filled with weapons. There were a couple of shotguns and handguns, several knives of varying sizes, switchblades, boot daggers, even a large axe. Aaron picked through the armory, examining each piece with fascination. He supposed it made sense that Eben would have all this equipment stashed away, given what he'd spent his life doing. But now, seeing the gleaming steel of the blades, handling the barrels of the guns, the unbelievable became real.

Eben — old, frail, loyal Eben — was a killer.

Aaron gritted his teeth. He opened his backpack and began to fill it with a couple of the knives and daggers. He considered the guns, then packed the 9mm. As he was putting the rest of the weapons back in the trunk, he noticed a wrapped package at the very bottom. Inside were half a dozen sticks of C4.

"Well, Eben, I'm glad you're prepared for everything," Aaron said as he stuck the explosives in his bag and zipped it shut. He dragged the trunk back into the closet and left the apartment, hoping he had left no obvious evidence of his presence.

At home, all Reggie could think of were those woods and what it meant that Henry had felt a weak presence. The rain had cleared, and the sun was going down. Reggie took off on her bike for the train trestle by the river.

When she got there she saw evidence that Quinn was still using the place as a hideout, but there was no sign of him. She waited for ten minutes, but she wanted to be home before dark and she still didn't know where he was. She found a piece of charred wood on the ground and left a note for Quinn written on one of the trestle's cement pylons.

Check out forest behind Thornwood.
May be V's new HQ.

She just prayed it wouldn't rain again before he got back.

18

Friday rolled around. June 20th. Reggie felt a heavy weight on her heart as she rose from bed. She had heard from neither Machen nor Quinn, and she knew nothing more about her enemies' plots to derail humanity. The summer solstice was the next day. She felt like a failure.

She and Aaron spent a couple hours at the local library, looking up county divisions, building permits, and land titles in the Thornwood area. They'd discovered that the hospital only owned a small portion of the land; the rest, some eighty acres of forest preserve, was was owned and managed by the state of Massachusetts.

"We could take Henry to the governor's mansion and see if he gets the heebie-jeebies," said Aaron as they walked back to Reggie's house in the afternoon. "My dad always said that guy looked shifty."

The TV's pale flashing light illuminated her home's living room window, and a single lamp shone up in Henry's room. In the quiet summer evening, scattered fireflies blinked among the yard's lengthening shadows. The world seemed calm and unaware of its impending doom, and Reggie had no idea what to do next. She wanted to contact Quinn, but after the motorcycle attack, he'd become a ghost again. She chuckled bitterly. Now, on the eve of the solstice, she was placing her hope in a Vour. Midsummer had already brought the world to madness.

"Check it out."

Aaron pointed to a rusted beige BMW idling a few yards past Reggie's house. They'd both ridden in it before.

Reggie raced up to the car and leant down by the passenger side window.

"Where have you been?" she asked Machen, who sat in the driver's seat.

"I've been waiting for you for hours. You had your cell phones turned off."

"Oh yeah, we were at the library," said Aaron, coming up behind Reggie.

"What's going on?" Reggie asked.

"I'll explain on the way. There isn't much time left. Hurry!"

Reggie shot a glance over to the living room window, then up to Henry's room. No one had seen her yet. She hopped in the passenger side and Aaron got in the back. He struggled out of his backpack's straps as the car gained speed.

No one spoke for the first several minutes. Reggie thought they were going to get on the highway, but Machen passed the exit and instead turned onto another country road farther down.

"Where are we going?" Reggie asked.

"We have to be careful when we all meet," Machen explained. "Vour spies are everywhere, and we can't risk being ambushed.

It would certainly make their year if they were able to take out the Tracer Council in one swoop."

"So we're going to meet the Council?" Aaron asked.

Machen nodded.

"This is important enough to warrant a gathering," he said, and glanced over at Reggie. "*You're* important enough."

"You said time is running out," said Reggie. "I'm honored to get into the Tracer clubhouse and everything, but can't the introductions wait until later?"

"Don't worry. We're here to help you." Machen made a hard left onto a dirt road.

Aaron kept glancing out the window and biting his lower lip. Wherever they were going, it didn't seem to be near civilization. They had passed a roadside bait-and-tackle shop some time ago and hadn't seen another building since. The car wove around the dirt roads through woods that were thinning out into farmland.

Eventually, Machen pulled off one of the narrow dirt roads and onto a gravel driveway that led up to an abandoned-looking farmstead. Reggie thought of Crazy Macie's old place, and goosebumps prickled her skin. Machen pulled up in front of the barn and stopped the car. The structure badly needed a coat of paint; its red color had faded to a dusty pink and was cracked all over.

They all got out. The barn door had a large padlock on its latch. Aaron went up and tugged at it, but it held fast.

"That's not for decoration," Machen said. He pulled a key out of his wallet and unlocked the door. It slid open to darkness.

"Looks like we're the first ones here," Reggie said.

Machen checked his watch.

"Yeah, that's a bit weird. The others were supposed to be here already. I hope nothing's happened. After you, guys."

Reggie entered first, then Aaron. It was pitch black inside.

"Hang on, there's a light switch here somewhere," said Machen, fumbling around the wall. "Ah, there we go."

Dim bulbs lit the barn. Empty horse stalls stood to one side and grain bins rose on the other. The place smelled of musty hay and pine.

"So what are we —" Reggie turned and stopped.

She and Aaron stared at Machen, who pointed a black semi-automatic handgun at them. His eyes were sad, but his hand was steady.

"I don't expect you guys to accept my apology," he said, "but I am sorry about this."

"You can't be one of them!" Reggie gasped.

"A Vour? Of course I'm not." He shook his head, but the gun stayed leveled at her. "It's like I told you, Reggie. You have a power no one understands yet. If you fall into the wrong hands — the Vours' hands — it could mean the end of us all."

"What are you talking about?" said Reggie. "I'm a threat to them. If I fall into their hands, they'll strangle me!"

"You're wrong," said Machen. "Your ability changes the game. We know it, and the Vours know it. They'll want to see if it can help them in some way."

"How?"

Machen cocked the pistol.

Reggie noticed a shadow move in the corner behind him.

"You don't know?" said Aaron. "You're going to kill us for something that *might* be true?"

"I have my orders." Machen's voice shook. "The risk is too great. We do what we have to do to win this war."

"The greater good," Reggie said.

Machen nodded. "You see it, don't you? I don't have a choice —"

A shape burst from the gloom beyond him, and Quinn Waters wrapped a length of baling wire around Machen's throat and pulled him off his feet. The older man crashed to the ground as the gun went off.

Quinn stomped on Machen's hand, forcing him to let go of the pistol, then kicked it away. Machen gagged as the wire tightened, cutting into his neck. He rammed his elbow into Quinn's ribcage, and a bone cracked. The Vour stumbled back, losing his grip on the garrote. Machen, gasping and purple-faced, sprang to his feet. He pulled the wire from around his throat. Quinn gained his footing just in time to receive a savage kick to the groin. He doubled over, and Machen attacked again, but Quinn shot up and struck Machen in the face with the back of his skull. Blood flowed from Machen's nose and mouth, and Quinn dove after him. The two grappled in the center of the barn.

"Holy shit!" Aaron yelled. *"Quinn!"*

Machen and Quinn continued to batter each other, both of them streaming with blood.

"Reggie!" shouted Aaron. "Get out of here!"

Reggie snatched the gun out of the dirt. She held it at her

side and watched the men fight, feeling both horrified and fascinated.

They had traveled to the other side of the barn, close to the grain silo. Quinn had Machen in a strangle hold, but Machen quickly flipped the Vour over his shoulder and hurled him to the floor. Quinn lay there for a second, the breath knocked out of him. Machen gave him a few solid kicks to the gut.

"Time to finish what Eben couldn't." Machen stood with his foot on Quinn's neck, poised to crush the life out of him.

But he didn't. Reggie and Aaron watched as Machen's foot trembled, and his face turned ghostly pale. He held his arms out in front of him like they were foreign bodies, and he gazed in horror at them.

"I know what you're afraid of," Quinn snarled. "And you have a weak heart."

Machen's face contorted in pain and he clutched his left arm. His legs gave out, and he fell heavily to the ground. His body went into convulsions. Quinn struggled to his feet and spat on Machen, his cold, green eyes wide and terrifying as he burrowed into the Tracer's mind.

"Stop it!" Reggie ran toward him.

Quinn took no notice. The labyrinth of black veins across his body pulsed and surged.

"Shoot him, Reg!"

Quinn laughed, though his eyes never moved from Machen's face. "Nah, your girl had the chance to kill me already and didn't."

Machen gasped and writhed on the floor. Reggie put her hand out and touched Quinn's arm.

"Please, stop."

Finally Quinn broke eye contact with his prey.

"Well, since you said please."

Reggie knelt down next to Machen and felt his pulse; it was weak, but he was breathing.

"He should be all right."

Quinn wiped his bloody nose on his forearm, and then rubbed his cracked rib.

"You want to *save* him? He was going to kill you."

"He doesn't deserve to die," Reggie said.

"He didn't feel the same way about you. You're both welcome, by the way. Cole, for Christ's sake, will you stop staring at me like I'm beefcake of the month?"

Aaron had been standing stock-still, gaping at the thing he thought he'd let die months earlier. The vision before him didn't compute in his logical mind.

"Come on, let's get out to the car — I'll explain on the way." Reggie grabbed Aaron's arm and pulled him along with her out of the barn.

"Reg, what's going on? We could at least shoot him in the thigh or something, incapacitate him until we get him to a cold enough place to get into his fearscape."

"Aaron, the situation's a little different than that."

"Different, how? You kill him or you save him, right?"

"Not this time."

Quinn stepped past the both of them and opened the driver's side door. He slid inside and reached for the keys dangling from the BMW's ignition.

"Time to go, kids. We've got a deadline."

Reggie grabbed the handle of the passenger door.

"Aaron, we've got to get going."

"With him? Have you fucking lost your mind?"

He crossed to Quinn's door and yanked it open.

"Get out of the car."

"Um, let me think. No."

"Reggie, give me the gun." Aaron stared icily at Quinn.

Reggie stood on the other side of the car and looked from one to the other of them.

"Aaron, I'm sorry."

"Oh, Reggie, you can't be . . ." He backed away from the car, his throat tightening.

"Aaron, he has information that will help us stop all this. Now get in the car. We have to get out of here." She climbed in the front seat, but Aaron didn't move.

"I am such an idiot. It was Quinn all along . . . the brain theories . . . and Thornwood . . . You've been talking to him this whole time, haven't you?" Aaron's mouth felt dry. "How could you trust him? How could you not tell me?"

"Because I knew you'd act this way about it." The words would sting, but there was no time to be gentle. "I needed to make a tough decision, and you were in such a state —"

"I was in a state?" Aaron was incredulous. He turned with fury. "Or was it that you were just too ashamed to tell me the truth?"

"Aaron." Reggie lowered her voice. "I'm sorry, but we need to get moving."

"It's him or me."

"We need him," she said. "I know you probably don't understand."

"I understand perfectly," Aaron said bitterly. "Maybe you can answer that question now. How keeping *this* from me was really protecting me."

"Jesus, Cole, do you need a Kleenex or a hug or what? Quit your whining and get in the car," said Quinn. "Or else hitch your way back. A cattle truck might pass by in a day or two."

Aaron looked furious, but he got in the backseat and Quinn started the engine. Soon they were winding their way back over the country roads toward Cutter's Wedge.

"You were wrong about one thing, Cole," Quinn said. "I didn't suspect Thornwood until Reg clued me in on it." He turned to her. "I got your note."

"And?"

"Oh yeah, there's something there. But it's not in a tree house. There's a whole network of tunnels and caves down there, definitely some freaky activity underway. We're going to have to hurry to get there in time."

"Then I hope you know your way back," Reggie said, gazing out at the winding road. "How did you get out here, anyway?"

"I've been tailing that guy for a while," Quinn replied. "I knew he was a Tracer, and those dudes are always bad news. Bunch of homicidal maniacs."

"That's funny, coming from you," Aaron muttered.

"Anyway, he'd been staking out your house all day," Quinn went on, ignoring Aaron. "I got suspicious, so when he ran for coffee I jimmied the trunk and hid inside."

"What happened in the barn?" Reggie asked. "Machen was about to kill you."

"Psychic attack. He let down his guard and I hit him with this nightmare he's been having since he was a little kid. Tree vines spring out of the ground and wrap around his whole body, and blah, blah, blah."

Quinn turned into Reggie and Aaron's neighborhood.

"No, not my house," said Reggie. "I can't risk —"

"We're not going to your house. We're going to *his*." Quinn jerked his head back toward Aaron.

"What? Why?" he asked.

"Hate to burst your bubble, but you're not exactly the super-soldier type, if you know what I mean. You better stay on the sidelines for this one."

"There's no way I'm letting Reggie go off alone with you."

"But Reggie's been alone with me plenty of times the last couple weeks, haven't you, Reg?"

Reggie just stared out the window. Aaron's fists clenched.

"You just don't get it, do you, Cole?" Quinn continued. "You're a liability. You'll put Reggie at risk if you come." He glanced up at Aaron in the rearview mirror, his green eyes radioactively bright. "You don't have the stones for this sort of work. Stick to the Internet and your library books. That's more your speed."

"It is not." Aaron's face was red with anger. "I can handle more than you think. Remember the lake, Quinn? I can deal with *you*."

Quinn parked and hopped out of the car.

"Sure you can." He opened Aaron's door and yanked him out by the shoulder.

Suddenly, Aaron was floating in the middle of the ocean, with no land in sight. He flailed his arms and kicked his legs trying to stay afloat, but he couldn't keep his head above the surface. Salty brine seeped into his mouth with every gasping breath. Shark fins, like giant black blades, cut circles through the water.

He told himself to push back, to resist, but the water still surrounded him. He tried to imagine dry land under his feet, to feel the solidity he knew was beneath him in reality, but found only the frigid depths. A great white shark with a Vour's black boiling eyes exploded from the waves in front of him. The monster's cave of teeth crashed down on him, and he screamed as the world turned red . . .

"See?"

Aaron lay sprawled on his lawn, clutching his chest and gasping. Quinn hovered over him and shook his head. Reggie pushed him aside and knelt down by her friend. He noticed Machen's gun tucked in her waistband.

"You've done everything you can do, Aaron. I know you feel betrayed. I didn't mean for it to happen this way. I didn't want you to have to deal with this — with him."

"Bullshit," Aaron gasped. "You sound like Eben."

He was right. She'd become what she loathed. But it was too late for regrets.

"If I don't come back, you and Eben need to finish this."

"You won't come back. You're a fool for trusting him, Reggie.

Don't go alone. Take me with you." Aaron tried to get up, but he was still too weak.

"You can't even stand, Aaron. What would happen if you came with me? You can't help me with this part. I'm sorry."

Reggie walked back to the passenger side and got in. Quinn glanced at him from the driver's seat and winked. Then he gunned the engine and the sedan sped off, leaving Aaron behind.

After he'd regained some of his strength, Aaron pedaled his bike furiously, the breeze cool against his sweat-soaked face. His lungs still burned from Quinn psychically drowning him, and his tailbone ached from when the Vour knocked him down. In the last hours of the day, a purple and gold sunset bruised the sky. His backpack, stuffed with the weapons he'd stolen, was slung over his shoulders, and he tried to keep from jostling it too much.

He could think of only one place to go, one person who could help him.

Aaron knew visiting hours would be over at the hospital, so he rode the elevator up and down until a group of doctors got off on the third floor. He followed them out, hiding behind them until he'd passed the nurses' station, then he sprinted down the corridor to Eben's room.

The light in the room was dim, and the old man was asleep. Aaron stood over him, marveling at how feeble he looked, with all the tubes poking in and out of him. His lips and nostrils were tinged black, giving the impression that he'd accidentally wiped pen ink across his face. Aaron hesitated — could this shell of a warrior really do anything to help him now?

Eben's eyes fluttered open. He did not look surprised to see Aaron.

"Come to see what living death looks like?" he asked.

"Eben, I . . ."

"Oh come, boy, spit it out," Eben said gruffly.

"It's bad. Reggie's just done about the stupidest thing in her whole goddamned life. And I couldn't stop her."

He told Eben what happened, and, by the time Aaron finished, the old man had already pulled the oxygen tube out of his nose and the IV out of his arm. He tried to stand but his balance was off, and Aaron had to catch him.

"Whoa, whoa, Eben. You can't go anywhere like this."

"Like hell I can't. Where did they go?"

"The forest preserve behind Thornwood Hospital. Something's back there, but I'm not sure what —"

"That's good enough. Get my clothes, would you? Showing up in one of these backless numbers won't inspire much fear in our enemies."

19

Black-barked trees towered over them, their thick canopy of leaves blocking out all but the slightest trace of the moon. They were driving down a path through the woods a few miles beyond Thornwood, and every once in a while Reggie could see a glimmer of the hospital's lights through the trees. Finally the brush grew too great, and Quinn parked the car.

"We'll have to walk from here," he said.

Reggie nodded and got out of the car. She kept the gun trained on Quinn with one hand and held the heavy black flashlight with the other. Quinn held up his hands.

"Oh come on, Halloway. You still don't trust me after all this?"

"Call me cautious," she replied, hoping Quinn didn't hear the quake in her voice.

"Just don't trip and shoot me by accident."

Quinn led the way through the tangled brush, cursing at the brambles as Reggie followed. An eerie hoot echoed through the darkness. Reggie knew an owl signified wisdom to the ancient Greeks, but medieval Europeans considered it a bad omen. She wondered which one it meant tonight.

They came to a clearing where the massive elms and oaks receded. Some rusted and vine-tangled sections of an iron gate surrounded it. Only a few saplings sprouted from a moonlit field. Among the weeds stood a scattering of mossy stones. Reggie shined her flashlight on one of them, and realized it was a grave marker.

"What is this place?" she asked.

"Potter's Field. It's where the asylum used to bury the dead patients if no one claimed their bodies," Quinn said. "Half of these graves are from botched lobotomies."

A ruined building not much bigger than a shed slouched in the dark meadow's corner. Quinn headed toward it. "The access point is over here."

"If I even *think* you're up to something funny, I'll shoot you in the head," Reggie said, though she prayed she wouldn't have to pull the trigger. Machen's gun felt weighty and awkward, and meant for a larger hand than hers.

"I got it, I got it."

Years of neglect had sagged the building's roof, and the bars over its windows were brown with corrosion. Lichen webbed its bricks, and tall grass rose from its cracked steps. A door made of rotting planks lay on the ground. The doorway stood open, and Quinn walked inside.

Reggie hesitated. She felt eyes on her, as if someone was watching her from the abandoned graveyard. She looked over her shoulder but saw only the shapes of the gravestones and nighttime forest beyond.

"You coming?" Quinn called back.

In horror movies, Reggie thought, this would be the point where she would yell at the screen for the heroine to just shoot the guy already and run. But she had come too far, and there was too much at stake.

She stepped inside the crumbling building and swung the flashlight's beam around. The floor was dirt, and a filthy puddle covered most of it. A rusty old mower leaned against the wall beside some broken rakes and a crumbling scythe. She tensed, half-expecting Quinn to run for one of them and come at her with it. He didn't.

Near the wall, under one of the barred windows, he squatted down and pulled back the locking bolt from a hinged manhole cover. Grunting and gasping, he yanked on the lid and swung it up off the concrete lip so that it stood vertically against the hinge.

"Presto," he said, gesturing at the hole. "Welcome to Hell."

Reggie cautiously waked over to him and looked into the hole. A ladder led down into darkness, moored into the walls of a concrete tunnel. It reminded her of the cavern in Keech's fearscape. She shuddered.

"I couldn't believe it when I found it. There are miles of access tunnels down there, a whole underground labyrinth," Quinn said, scratching his head. "You could get lost and never find your way out again."

"I wish for once the mad scientists would do their experiments at the beach. I could get a tan *and* fight evil." Reggie gestured to the hole. "You first. I'll be right behind you, so don't do anything stupid."

"I think we'd both agree going down there is pretty stupid," Quinn replied, but he lowered himself into the hole and began to descend.

Reggie realized she would not be able to climb down the ladder holding both the gun and the flashlight, so she slid the pistol's safety on and secured the flashlight in the waistband of her pants.

She hurried down after him, resting the wrist of her gun-hand on the rungs to steady herself as she grabbed them with the other. It was dark and getting colder. The passage's mouth was a deep gray circle against black, shrinking overhead as she went down.

"*Ow*, my fingers, watch it!" Quinn snarled. "You're right on top of me."

The air grew damper, and the rungs became slippery as they went deeper.

"How much farther?" she said.

"About ten feet or so," he panted from below. "I hate this place. Wet and cold." He grunted. "Okay, I'm at the bottom now."

Reggie thought she must have just a few rungs left, but then her boot slipped off the ladder and she pitched backward. She tried to hang on with her empty hand, but the bar was slick and her feet couldn't find the next rung. Her fingers slid off and she fell to the ground, jarring her knee. The gun clattered out of her hand and skidded across the floor. She heard Quinn chuckle, and his footsteps echoed in the darkness. Reggie scrambled to her feet.

She swung the flashlight back and forth, but the beam didn't go very far, and Quinn was nowhere in sight. Her breath quickened. A tunnel of moldering cement stretched out in either direction, with dank water dripping from the ceiling and pooling on the floor. A creaking, followed by an echoing boom, came from above. Reggie shone the light up the ladder. The manhole cover had fallen back into place. She willed herself to believe it had happened on its own, and not that someone else had pushed it.

Black terror blossomed in her chest. She heard a noise and whirled around, shining the flashlight down the left tunnel. Quinn stood ten feet away with the gun in his hand, pointing it at her.

They'd had to wait until the nurses were distracted, then Aaron helped Eben to the elevator. He was about to press the ground floor button, but Eben stopped him.

"Lower level parking lot," he grunted. Even with his cane he had to lean against the wall to stand. His broken arm rested in a sling.

"Uh, you didn't drive yourself here, Eb. Your car's at home."

"But there must be *a* car in the parking lot, don't you think? How did you expect to get us out to Thornwood? I can't very well ride on the back of your bicycle."

The doors opened and Eben limped out. The lot wasn't full since it was evening, but a black sedan was parked down the ramp, out of sight from the cashier's stand.

"That will do," Eben said, and holding Aaron's arm for support, they walked slowly toward the car.

"Do you have anything heavy in that backpack of yours?" Eben asked.

Aaron swallowed guiltily.

"Er . . . well . . ."

Faster than Aaron would have thought possible for a man with one good arm, Eben had grabbed the pack and unzipped it. He shook his head at Aaron.

"Eben, I'm sorry. I thought maybe something in your apartment would help us —"

"Later." Eben cut him off. "As it turns out, this wasn't the dumbest move you've ever made, by a very slim margin." He took out the 9mm, checked that the safety was on, and smashed the butt against the back window behind the driver's seat. The window shattered, but louder than that was the BEEP BEEP BEEP of the car's alarm.

In an instant Eben had reached his uninjured hand through and unlocked the driver's door, then slid into the seat and pulled out the car alarm wires beneath the steering column. The beeping stopped. The whole thing had taken about seven seconds.

Eben leaned back in the seat and looked in the rearview mirror. No one was coming. He reached down and fumbled around with more wires, and the car engine roared to life.

Aaron was slack-jawed.

"You're going to teach me how to do that someday, right?"

"Aaron, get in the car."

Quinn started walking toward her, holding out the gun. Reggie stood completely still, her jaw set. He was going to shoot her, and she deserved it for her stupidity.

But then he took the gun with his other hand, grasping it by the barrel. He held it out to her again, this time with the butt facing her. He waved it at her.

"Go ahead, take it."

Reggie's eyes darted back and forth. Was this a trick? She reached out and grabbed the gun, expecting Quinn to pull it away, teasing her, but he let it go as soon as her fingers were wrapped around it.

"I told you you could trust me, Reggie," he said. "Now let's stop wasting time. They should be this way."

He started down the tunnel, and Reggie followed, her heart pounding.

The tunnel wound dizzily through the underground, and divided often in sudden forks. When they came to these Quinn would hover by each branch before choosing one of them. Reggie had lost all sense of direction.

"How do you know which one to take?" she asked after the fourth or fifth divergent path. "Can you sense other Vours?"

"I can sense fear," he answered, "and we're getting close to some pretty petrified humans."

Are you sure that's not me? Reggie thought, but she didn't say anything.

She could hear new noises now, besides the constant dripping water. Far off groans and wails. It could be wind through the tunnels, or it could be something more alive . . .

"How much farther?"

"Not much. Look."

Quinn pointed, and Reggie could see dim lights protruding

from the cave walls. Quinn put his hand over the flashlight, shielding its beam.

"Better turn that off."

Reggie nodded and clicked off the light. They went forward more slowly now, and the moans got louder. Reggie started to gag on the air: a new, wretched odor lingered with the scent of moisture and mildew. It was the smell of rotting flesh.

Suddenly the narrow tunnel widened; candle sconces provided weak light and flickering shadows on the wall. The stench was almost unbearable as they came upon a cage built into the side of the passage.

"This is pure fear." Quinn pointed to the cage, and Reggie peered between the bars, trying not to breathe in. She need not have worried; the horror closed her throat.

Lying on the ground in putrid rags was a middle-aged woman. Her head was shaved and a large scar ran up across her forehead and over her crown. It looked like it had been stitched up hastily, and greenish pus oozed from the wound. She rocked back and forth on the wet earth, and Reggie saw a tube extend from her arm up into an IV bag hanging from the wall. The bag was filled with black sludge, and it was pumping into her veins. Where the needle was injected on her forearm a black rash spidered across her skin.

Quinn was looking in a folder attached to the bars of the cage.

"It's her medical chart," he said.

"What are they doing to her?" Reggie gasped.

"They're feeding her . . . ew . . . they're feeding her Vour essence."

"They're *what*?"

"Like that thing you ate. To get your powers? They're feeding a liquid version to her. Only it's having rather worse effects, I'd say."

Suddenly the woman hopped to her feet and started screaming incoherently. She ran at the bars of her cage, and before Reggie could jump back, she grabbed her hands and clenched them tightly. Reggie tried to pull away, but the manic woman's grip was too strong. She shrieked, opening her mouth so wide it looked like her jaw was unhinged, and Reggie saw that her teeth and tongue were black, and the whites of her eyes were crisscrossed with dark lines. She tried to bite Reggie's thumb, but Quinn grabbed Reggie by the shoulders and heaved her away. They fell back onto the ground, and the woman started banging her head on the iron bars so hard it lacerated her skin. With blood dripping down her temples, she collapsed onto the floor again.

Reggie gasped for breath as Quinn stood and helped her to her feet.

"I guess that's what happens to some people when they eat Vour," he said. "Consider yourself truly blessed."

They continued down the tunnel, which Reggie realized was a corridor in a kind of dungeon. They passed cell after cell, all filled with victims of the Vours' cruelty. Some had electrodes strapped to their bodies and were intermittently shocked with electricity; others were, like the first woman, being fed various concoctions of Vour and other toxins. Many were lobotomized; Quinn read a couple charts that showed human brains being partially replaced with Vours'. These patients were mostly catatonic, lying in a state of stupor; however, Reggie could see their eyes darting back and forth behind their closed eyelids, and she wondered what horrors their minds were seeing and could not escape from.

"This would mean that they're sacrificing Vours as well as humans," she said to Quinn.

"Of course," he replied. "Omelets and eggs, you know. The greater good."

Reggie almost laughed, though it was far from funny. The greater good had been Eben's and Machen's excuse for the atrocities they'd committed, as well.

The cages went on and on. Men, women, the elderly, the young. They were so starved some had eaten their own tongues, and all of them smelled like death. Reggie wanted to close her eyes but she forced herself to look, forced herself to know what her enemy was capable of, and how high the stakes were should they succeed.

Each cage had its own chart and pictures like the ones Quinn had shown her of the brain. In some the amygdala remained small, in some it was larger, but none that were dated recently showed it as big as it was on the winter solstice. So far, all of the Vours' experiments had failed. Reggie took what comfort she could from this.

She thought she saw something move out of the corner of her eye, and she glanced at the wall. It seemed to oscillate in and out, pushing in toward her and then pulling away again. The effect made her dizzy, and she felt herself sway. She saw veins and sinews pop out of the sides of the tunnel, and the ground suddenly felt squishy beneath her feet, like she was walking on muscle tissue instead of earth.

She reached out to Quinn to steady herself.

"What's happening?" she asked.

"You're in the belly of the beast," he replied. "What'd you expect to see?"

Reggie's heart lurched; his voice was low and sinister, like how he had sounded when he had kidnapped her last December. She struggled to push the visions away, to turn the esophagus she was in back into earthen tunnels. The veins began to turn back to rock, the fleshy ground to dirt. But then Quinn grabbed her by the arm and tossed her forward. She had the sensation of the room opening up around her as she stumbled to the ground, and then she heard the clanging of metal. Instantly the nightmare vanished, and Reggie saw that Quinn had locked her in her own cage.

"You asshole," she spat.

"You idiot," he retorted, and he grinned at her, the malicious sneer that she remembered so well. "I mean, I know I'm good, but even I wondered if you'd be so gullible." He shook his head. "If it makes you feel any better, I did actually come to you for help initially. But when I saw how easy it was going to be to get you to trust me, I knew I had the ultimate bargaining chip to win back favor with the family."

"Why didn't you just kill me?"

Quinn laughed. "That was the genius of it! They never wanted you dead! That Gale thing? That was all for show. 'Course, they weren't expecting me to kill her, but that was for your benefit."

"And Keech? Keech was a plant, too?"

"Hell no." Quinn held up the hand that was missing two fingers. It was still black from being doused in the river. "You think I would have let him do this? Keech was under orders to kill me, but after that day in the theater, I knew I had you. And then I made my deal. Bring you in, alive and screaming. And believe me, you will scream."

The gun was still in her hand. Reggie raised it, the barrel pointed directly at Quinn's chest on the other side of the bars.

"One for you and one for me," she said. "They'll have to take me dead."

She pulled the trigger. The gun clicked.

She tried again, but again, no shot. She checked the safety — it was off. The gun had jammed.

She heard Quinn's low chuckle and looked up at him. He held out his palm, and in it was the gun's clip.

"Amateur," he snarled.

Heavy thuds sounded far away down the tunnel. The footsteps of an army. Quinn's eyes twinkled.

"They're coming."

The candles blew out, leaving the cave in darkness. The footsteps grew louder, then Reggie felt a pain in her arm. Her legs grew weak beneath her, and she flopped to the ground in a deep sleep.

The first thing she felt was a tremendous ache in her temple, like a drill bearing down over her left brow. She struggled to open her eyes, but it took several moments for her vision to clear. She tried to move her hands and feet, but she could not feel them. Whatever drug they had given her had paralyzed her from the neck down.

Slowly Reggie took in her bearings. She was in a larger space now, and she was strapped to a stone slab tilted at a sixty-degree angle. She saw that her wrists were lashed so tightly with cord that they were bleeding, but she couldn't feel a thing.

"Welcome back, my dear," said a voice behind her. She thought it sounded familiar, but she could not place it. She tried to turn her head, but a searing pain shot through it from ear to ear. For the first time she realized a giant needle was sticking out of her forehead. She felt her breath constrict — what was this?

"Ah, ah, careful there," the voice continued. "It will hurt less if you remain still, Miss Halloway."

"I know you. Who are you?" Reggie croaked. Her vocal cords felt loose, and her lips had trouble properly forming words.

"I'm someone who's helped you. And now it's time for you to help me." A figure walked around the slab and his face came into view.

"Dr. Unger." Reggie's addled mind tried to compute what she was seeing. It *was* the doctor, but he couldn't be a Vour. Henry had been so sure. "I don't understand. You're not . . . not . . ."

"Not one of them? No, I'm merely a human. I have not the gift to telepathically inspire fear. My methods are far more crude."

"Then why —?"

"Why do all this? I'm a scientist, Miss Halloway. And the existence of Vours has proven to be one of the most fascinating discoveries in our world's history. They want to know the same things I want to know, so it is a unique partnership, you see."

"Why didn't they Vourize you?" Reggie rasped.

"I think they find it, shall we say, advantageous to have a few like-minded humans in their fray. Tracers, for example, would not come after me — even the most cursory investigation would prove I was human. I can carry on my work, *our* work, with impunity. But that is enough chatter. The hour is getting late, and we have much to do."

Unger clapped his hands, and the lights in the cavern grew brighter. Reggie could see more clearly now; she was in an underground chamber shaped like an octagon, and stone slabs like the one she lay upon stretched out in rows in front of her. Comatose humans were strapped to these, all with needles jutting out of their heads, and these were connected to each other with tubes and wires.

Reggie followed the length of the wires with her eyes and saw that they flowed to her bed, and that she in turn was attached to a series of television monitors. Each monitor showed a live scan of a brain.

"What are you going to do to me?"

"It's not what I'm going to do to you. It's what you're going to do to *him*."

Unger gestured to the cavern entrance, where two hospital orderlies were supporting a body into the room.

"Quinn! Our loyal soldier!"

The orderlies led Quinn up to Unger and Reggie, and at first, Reggie thought the light must be playing tricks on her. Quinn's skin looked blue, almost purple, and his eyelashes and nostrils were covered with little crystals. He was so weak he could not stand on his own.

"Y-y-you s-s-son of a-a b-b-b-bitch," he stuttered through chattering teeth. "F-f-freezer . . . l-l-eft me th-there . . ."

"Yes, of course. How else will Miss Halloway enter your — what does she call it? Your fearscape."

Quinn shrank away, but the burly orderlies held him fast.

"W-why? I h-h-helped y-you."

"Yes, you did. And now you're going to make the ultimate sacrifice for the good of your kind. They'll write sonnets about you, Quinn — that is, they will if there are any humans left who know how to write them."

"Omelets and eggs, Quinn," Reggie muttered.

The orderlies strapped Quinn to his own berth right next to Reggie's, then jabbed a needle into his forehead. Quinn screeched in pain, and even Reggie shuddered as she heard the point crack through his skull. She thought of the needle in her own head and felt faint. But why did they want her to go into Quinn's fearscape? Did they want her to fail and die? Or did they want her to succeed?

Unger seemed to read her thoughts.

"There is something special about you, my dear. To have ingested that poison and not been driven completely insane — I don't know how you did it, but I know that it makes you the key. Your ability to pass through dimensions whenever you choose — it is remarkable. The Vours have been trying to do it for years. Now you will show us how."

He undid the cord around Reggie's lifeless hand and pressed her fingers to Quinn's wrist, right on his pulse. Then he retied their hands together that way, securing them tightly. She could not feel Quinn's icy skin, but her eyes lost focus as her mind tumbled down into the realm of nightmare . . .

20

. . . and she was standing on a narrow, cracked sidewalk just a short distance outside Cutter's Wedge Elementary. The grassy fields that sprawled around the real school did not exist in this realm. Instead of plants and shrubs, dense and motionless blobs surrounded the building. There was no playground, no parking lot, no grove of tall pine trees in the distance — only layers of thick, bland gunk that looked like cake icing polluted with molten lead.

Just off the path, a long wooden board with a cracked red seat and plastic handle poked out of the gunk like a utensil in a jar of gray honey. Other playground objects had been caught in the substance as well — a tetherball pole, a swing set, a faded basketball backboard. Nothing moved.

Reggie walked slowly down the path to the school's front entrance, the once concrete sidewalk squishing beneath her feet like moss. Something about the nature of this place was different from the outer layers of Henry's and Keech's fearscapes. Reggie did not sense immediate fear here. She'd learned enough from her previous jaunts into these forsaken places to trust her instincts, but right now her psychic compass was unresponsive. This outermost region of Quinn's fearscape seemed no longer *functional*.

Small, colorless hands reached out from the goop near the stone steps leading to the front doors of the building. Reggie knelt in front of the stairs and saw the remnants of faces swirled and frozen inside the strange matter like paint strokes. Everything here had come undone.

Reggie stretched out and touched the grayness beyond the sidewalk, and the tips of her fingers bled out all color and went numb. She withdrew her hand and held it up to her face. The color returned to her fingertips and she could feel them again.

"It's like he's forgotten this place."

At the sound of her voice a barely perceptible tremor pulsed through the sidewalk. One of the tiny hands in the ooze twitched. She stood again carefully and climbed the steps, avoiding the few gaps in them that revealed more gray substance below.

Reggie stepped inside the doors. Square gray tiles covered the floor in this version of Cutter's Wedge Elementary. It looked like a photo negative of reality with light and dark reversed. A monochrome banner hung at the corridor's end, tattooed with the giant face of Bucky, the cheery pirate mascot that Reggie remembered from her school days here.

The banner was emblazoned with rows of jagged and indecipherable symbols in place of school spirit slogans. At the far end of the hallway, she saw the distant double doors of the gym. The walls of the hall were syrupy and looked as if they were quietly melting away. The same strange, gray matter covered them, but inside the building the gunk was not entirely static.

None of the levels of the fearscapes she'd seen yet had this appearance, this feeling of nothingness just beyond the immediate sights. Reggie wondered if it had been years since the Vour had scared a young Quinn deeper into the pit, and if these layers were degrading with time.

A low groan echoed behind her, and Reggie looked back.

Bucky the mascot's huge, disembodied pirate head floated down the hallway toward her, its chin a few feet over the tiles, the top of its hat barely clearing the ceiling.

The eye patch on the pirate's giant face had fallen, and the gaping eyeless hole opened and closed like a primitive mouth. The effect was almost comical, but it would have mortified an eight- or nine-year-old child, and that raw fear gave it power.

She ran, grabbing and pulling on classroom door handles as she passed, and each one crumbled or broke off in her hand. One near the end of the hall opened, and Reggie rushed to get inside, realizing too late that there was no room beyond the door.

Instead the floor dropped away into an ocean of gray. Reggie grabbed the doorframe just in time, catching herself before she plummeted off the edge. Then something snatched her right ankle and dragged her back into the hall.

An oily creature like a gigantic earthworm slithered out of the pirate's eye, and now its pin-teeth bit down on her leg. Reggie twisted her torso to face the worm and kicked its maw with her free foot.

The greasy thing let up and Reggie yanked her leg out of its mouth, tiny black teeth ripping from the soft tissue and clinking on the tile like loose change. She scrambled backward, rushed to her feet, and raced to the next door in the hall.

When she pulled it open, the space on the other side was solid, and she stepped onto cool, wet grass. The door slammed shut behind her and disappeared.

A ferocious growl shook the air, and two massive paws tromped down in front of her. Reggie looked up at an enormous bear standing at its full height, its thick, dark fur bristling and its razor sharp claws dripping with black ooze.

A disembodied voice seemed to echo from the sky.

"The western grizzly shows no mercy to its prey, preferring human flesh above all else," the voice said, and Reggie dimly recognized it as the narrator from PBS nature documentaries. "It rips its victim's skin from its body, and eats the still-living tissue beneath. If there are cubs, they too will feed."

The beast lashed out at her. Reggie rolled to the side just as the bear's front paws slammed to the ground and gouged out a chunk of dirt. She clambered toward a tattered tent, the only object in sight that could serve as a potential portal to a deeper fearscape region. The bear lumbered after her, but she reached the tent in time and dove through the dirty nylon entrance.

Inside, a small child huddled in the corner, wrapped in a threadbare blanket with his head bowed. Reggie crouched down and approached him.

"Quinn?"

At the sound of her voice, the blanket flew off and what Reggie thought was a boy jerked its head up to reveal a horrific face. Two drill bits protruded from where the thing's eyes should have been, whirring in the ragged sockets. A buzz saw had been affixed with leather straps to the stump of each severed wrist, and rusted spikes protruded from various holes in his chest. A giant fly's mandibles twitched in place of lips. Reggie cupped a hand over her mouth and slowly backed out of the tent.

The landscape had changed again, and she stood in a chamber of limbless and headless human torsos that had been gutted, cleaned, and now swayed from meat hooks on chains that led up into darkness. Fuzzy clumps of mold formed on the slicks of blood across the floor. The warehouse was a boiling cloud of flies; filthy legs and wings tickled her skin.

Reggie frantically pushed her way through the hanging meat slabs as the insect-child clacked its mandibles and followed, its bristly insect mouth buzzing. Swarming mites roiled around her eyes and mouth, and she gagged on their little bodies as she scrambled away. The monster's fly mouth undulated, and the eye socket drills whirred left and right as it pursued her.

She hit a dead end and turned around just as the buzzing saws of the monster's arms sliced the air in front of her, but before it could cut her, the bear appeared between them and swiped at the child-thing with its mammoth paw.

The bear shredded the insect-thing to pieces, and black, greasy liquid sprayed out of the mutilated body. The bear then grabbed the decapitated insect head, opened its huge, salivating mouth, and swallowed it whole.

Within seconds, the animal's face contorted, and the bear

unleashed an ear-shattering howl as it morphed into a new demonic entity. The drill bits pushed out through the bear's eye sockets with disgusting pops and whirs. The clicking mandibles cracked through the jaw, and the claws of the beast split open to make room for the whirling saws that grew out of its paws. The transformation was so shocking that Reggie stood frozen for a few seconds, before running back through the dense grove of body parts, trying not to scream.

As horrifying as Keech's and Henry's fearscapes had been, Reggie had navigated her way through both by finding a pattern, some internal and disturbing logic that tied the elements together.

But what was *this*?

First a wasteland outside the school, and now a layer inside the building with severely disjointed imagery and mutating, cannibalistic things. The fearscape was literally *eating* itself.

And as the deadly mutation chased her, tearing down torsos from chains as it stalked its new prey, the revelation struck her like lightning.

Quinn's fears here are merging.

The outermost layer had atrophied and simply stopped moving. Whatever fear had created the schoolyard environment, it had long been forgotten. And now this inner realm was blending together. She was not inside one layer but *many*, and over time they had bled into each other the same way human memory was prone to do. There was no twisted logic, no demented sense of order here. Quinn's brain had combined diverse layers of his fearscape and created a new breed of horror, one ravaged by absolute chaos.

Reggie reached the edge of the hanging carnage and gazed out in desperation at the utter destruction of downtown Cutter's Wedge. Entire buildings had been reduced to smoldering piles of steel and stone, fires burned inside guts of cars, and the sky above glowed a deep, frightening crimson.

Reggie thought of the things she had seen. The bear, a subject of a frightening nature show. A boy whose body parts had been replaced with dangerous, violent tools. A meat locker. A war.

Real terrors a young boy had feared many years ago, and here they converged into one jungle of pure mayhem.

A dozen or more "survivors" stumbled into the street in front of Reggie. Men, women, and children, they looked like walking corpses, burnt skin suppurating from their bodies and dripping onto to the glass-littered asphalt. Their eyes had been melted away, their sockets bloody and filled with pus as they staggered toward Reggie.

"Help me . . ."

"Please . . ."

Suddenly, the mutated bear-thing stomped on a burning car behind her. Reggie ran to the curb as the beast pounced upon the gaggle of walking dead. It snatched up a child and devoured it. But before it could catch a second meal, the other victims fell upon it and dragged it to the ground. Reggie did not stay to see the slaughter, nor what new abomination would arise from it.

She hurried off down the scorched street and soon saw the double doors of the school gymnasium ahead of her. They seemed to be the only symbol of some perverse continuity.

Enter those doors and find a deeper fearscape layer.

Go deeper, and you get closer to Quinn.

She heard footsteps behind her: the new mutation, this one part human, part bear, part buzz saw, sped toward her. It ran on legs half covered with fur, half with blackened, peeling skin, its saw hands spinning, its bear fangs gnashing. Reggie threw open the doors and dashed onto the cool gymnasium floor. The doors slammed behind her just as the new beast banged into them. It could not enter; it had reached some invisible boundary. Like the killer clown and the surgeon from Henry's fearscape, monsters from the domain's outer layers could not break from their psychic tethers and cross over here.

Should she fail in her attempt to save Quinn, Reggie imagined the gym she now occupied would also merge into the outer layers beyond and add to the chaotic canvas of mixed fears.

For now, she was the only one who could pass, and she had just entered a deeper and more defined level.

A washed-out sepia tone bathed the entire gym. Pudgy and awkward boys dressed in oversized uniforms ran laps around the basketball court. Huge wind-up keys protruded from their backs, constantly rotating in gaping red wounds between their shoulders.

An enormous man dressed in dark green bike shorts, black wrestling shoes, and a yellow windbreaker stood in the center of the gym, his broad back to Reggie. He stood in the middle of a blue wrestling mat that was covered in hundreds of tiny, sharp spikes. He blew a loud and shrill whistle, and the jogging children froze and huddled together on the perimeter of the court.

"Eagan! Lindsay! Get your sorry asses out on the mat!"

Reggie recognized the voice, even though she couldn't see his face. Mr. Banner had spent decades as the Cutter's Wedge Elementary gym teacher before finally being fired for slapping an asthmatic student who refused to run. Reggie was a first grader at the school when Banner had been terminated; she'd barely known him. Quinn, on the other hand . . .

"Let's go!"

Several of the boys squirmed and bustled before expelling two peers out from their midst. One was squat and doughy with short blond hair, the other one lanky and pale with big ears and shaggy brown locks. The whistle blew again.

"Move it! Don't make me get out the medicine ball again, boys! You remember what happened to Hyatt, don't you?" The coach pointed to a large puddle of dried maroon fluid that stained the wood floor beneath one of the baskets. A flayed body dangled upside-down from the rim above.

"Move your lazy tails!"

The two boys walked onto the mat, shooting one another nervous glances. The coach put his hands to his hips.

"You two are buds, aren't you? Little playmates, right? Don't think I don't see you giggling like girls and playing grab-ass in my class. I don't take kindly to gigglers and grab-assers. Assume the position, girls. Eagan, down!"

The skinny boy slowly dropped to his knees, the little spikes of the gym mat pushing up into them. He grimaced and placed his palms down after, and Reggie heard the sickening squish as the points penetrated his hands. She knew the boys didn't exist — they were grotesque figments of young Quinn's imagination, but they had been molded from the clay of actual memory. Somewhere, sometime, there was a real Eagan who suffered torment at the hands of Coach Banner while Quinn and others watched.

"Top, Lindsay. Get your flabby butt in position."

The chubby boy sank to one knee, wrapped his left arm underneath the other boy's stomach, and placed his right hand on his opponent's right elbow.

"Wrasslin', girls! This is what it's all about! A true man's sport! Now when I blow the whistle, you two best go at it full boat until one of you scores, you hear me? I catch either of you grab-assing out on my mat and I will tan some hides! Am I clear?"

The whistle blew a third time, and the chubby boy yanked hard on the skinny boy's arm. The elbow bent out at a frightening and distorted angle, and the boy tilted and collapsed on his side. The spikes pierced the full side of his emaciated body, and rivulets of black ooze poured out of dozens of puncture wounds around his ribs and hips. The chubby boy hesitated.

"Come on, Lindsay! Show us you're not a wuss!" The gym coach kicked the boy in the backside. "Take him! Pin his scrawny butt! You want to be an athlete? You want to be a man?"

The chubby boy's lips quivered.

"Where the hell is Waters? Quinn Waters! Get your butt out here and show these nerds how a champion competes!"

Reggie felt her heart race from her perch behind the bleachers. Was Quinn really that close? The gym teacher, the mat, the court, the boys in the class — all seemed to be well intact, suggesting enough of Quinn's essence was somewhere near. His living fear fed this scene enough to let it play out again and again in the fearscape. But Quinn did not appear.

"Damn it! Waters, I know you hear me! You goddamn quitter! Just like your old man! All the talent in the world and no guts!"

Reggie felt a twinge of pity, guessing that a young Quinn Waters had been pushed and pressured by adults around him to succeed as an athlete at any cost.

The coach stalked across the mat and shoved Lindsay to the side. Then he lifted his foot and stomped on Eagan's head, crushing it like a rotten watermelon. It splintered against the metal pikes, and more oily black fluid gushed across the mat. It wasn't blood but neither was it the smoke Reggie found inside the children in Henry's fearscape version of the carnival.

Perhaps over time, some layers solidified more than others? Reggie wondered.

Banner lifted his foot again to crush Lindsay, but Reggie gasped audibly, and the coach turned to the bleachers. To Reggie's horror and disgust, the thing had no face. It looked like someone had taken a surgical scalpel and carved out the fullness of Banner's visage, cut through flesh, muscle and bone, drained all blood and mucus, and then scooped out tissue and brain until nothing remained but a hollowed-out cove.

The only thing inside now was a bright, silver whistle clamped between a set of stained teeth molded to the pulpy back of his pinkish head.

"Sounds like we got a spy in here, boys!" The teeth opened and closed slightly as the monstrous gym teacher yelled and stomped toward the bleachers, puffs of unseen air tweeting the whistle a little with every step. "You best come out, dirty little spy."

He kicked some of the wooden slats and listened. Reggie stayed deathly still.

"That crotchety, used-up Munson sent you over from Wennemack to scout out my team this year, right? Figures that old bastard would stoop to cheating. Couldn't take a Banner crew any season, no matter how many spies he's got! Boys! You ferret me out our spy and I'll cut you loose on laps for the rest of the day!"

The boys murmured excitedly among themselves.

"Get a move on, boys, or I'll stitch you into the medicine ball!"

The group of timid kids charged at the bleachers like a pack of wild dogs. Reggie bolted out from behind the stands toward the hallway, but the path she'd taken into the gym had disappeared. There was no exit, and the boys laughed as they surrounded her.

She darted across the center of the gym, and the spikes of the mat punctured her feet. A couple of the boys tried to follow her, but they tripped and landed on the spikes with dull, wet splatters.

"That girl is schooling you, Tolin! Get your ass in gear, boy! Don't let her touch my medicine ball!"

Reggie reached the equipment closet and found it unlocked. She yanked the door closed behind her and wedged a hockey stick against the handle. The boys pounded on the door. She had only moments to find a way out before they'd be upon her.

Reggie desperately searched the closet for something useful. She clawed through the carts of basketballs, rows of orange cones, stacked floor-hockey nets, and grabbed hold of an aluminum bat. It felt solid and heavy in her hand.

The boys broke down the door and Reggie struck. Skulls broke open and filled the room with black ooze before bodies vanished in a poof of smoke. But the children kept coming at her, forcing her to retreat to the back of the closet, where she bumped into something warm and soft. And wet. It groaned.

Banner's medicine ball.

The sphere was three feet in diameter, made from a leathery canvas sewn together from the hides of dozens of young boys once tortured students in Banner's class. The same fresh black fluid dripped from the seams, and the morbid ball felt torturously alive.

The coach's whistle blew so loud and shrill that the heads of the remaining boys exploded in smoke, and their bodies tumbled forward and dropped to the ground.

Banner stalked inside the closet, his meaty concave head throbbing with anger. He had Reggie trapped.

"You take your hands off that ball, little girl."

He snatched a hockey puck from a shelf and hurled it at Reggie. The puck slammed into the back wall and cracked through the other side.

"Roll it to me now and I'll kill you quick."

A soft light poured through the rift in the wall behind Reggie. The other side was the way out. She pounded her fist against it as Banner grabbed a hockey stick with a glinting razor-edged blade.

"Disobey, and I'll bleed you slow."

Reggie placed both hands on the medicine ball. Dozens of pained faces, stitched together, stared up at her, and she felt the children's skins pulsing hot beneath her fingertips.

She picked the ball up over her head.

"No! Put it down, you little bitch!"

Reggie heaved it into the wall behind her. The barrier bowed and warped before collapsing away. Reggie was bathed in a deep orange glow, and the equipment closet around her washed away. The screaming gym teacher split apart into strips of clayish flesh and black ooze, and then Reggie sensed herself falling, unable to see anything but the fog around her.

When the haze cleared, she stood on the edge of a quiet cornfield that extended in all directions for as far as she could see. Behind her was nothing but swirling gray mist. She stared at the innocent-looking terrain before her.

"So what fun secrets are you hiding?" she asked the stalks. "Killer creamed corn?" She walked into the amber field.

21

Unger watched with barely concealed glee as the television monitors began to beep and blip with electrical waves from Reggie's and Quinn's brains. Data streamed across the screens and the brain images lit up with color as blood flowed to both their amygdalas. Quinn moaned and twitched, but the movement was slight, and their hands stayed in contact.

Reggie's neuron centers grew larger every second — Unger had never seen anything like it. Her emotional response to whatever she was facing in Quinn's fearscape was off the charts, as were her serotonin levels. Furthermore, areas of her brain not usually functional in human beings were lighting up like Christmas trees as the neuro-pathways rearranged themselves. Unger was seeing activity he had never known could exist.

This girl was the catalyst, he felt sure of it. She was like a battery that could jump-start a car, only she'd be jump-starting other human brains, overloading their amygdalas with emotional energy that would blow them up and demolish the gate that stood between the Vour world and this one. Vours would be able to cross over anytime, any day.

"It is going to happen!" he shouted into the cavern. Vours of all ages, posing as men, women, boys, and girls, began to swarm into the room and stood among the prostrate human bodies. They smiled devilishly and applauded the doctor.

"You have done well by us," said one.

"When will the rest come through?" asked another.

"Soon." Unger strode to a switch coupled to the nexus of wires. "When I connect them, her power will ignite all the hosts."

He flipped the switch, and a jolt of electricity surged through all the wires, which sparked and sizzled. The unconscious human victims spasmed as the current shot through them. On the television screens, their brain images began to show the same activity as Reggie's, though the neuron firings were not as strong. Unger watched the screens carefully.

"It's working. As she grows stronger in the fearscape, so do these hosts. The moment the fearscape implodes, the barrier will be eclipsed." Unger laughed. "The girl's power to defeat the Vours will be what liberates them!"

Suddenly an explosion shook the cavern, and an expanse of the dirt ceiling caved in on the gathered group. Balls of flame and dirt rained down from above, threatening to set the whole room ablaze. Shots rang out, and two Vours fell to the ground, dead. Black fumes gushed from their lips and eyes, mingling with the smoke from the fire.

Unger attempted to shield Reggie and Quinn with his body, watching the wires attached to their brains. He could not risk them going up in flames, not when Reggie was so close to conquering the fearscape.

A dagger flipped through the air and hit an orderly in the stomach. Unger jumped back as the Vour crumpled to the ground.

Flames sprouted all around the cavern. The Vours scattered, and some caught fire as they tried to flee. Billows of black smoke choked the room as earth and rock poured in from above. Still the red neuron hives on the television screens swelled.

"Almost there, almost there," Unger chanted.

"Back away from the girl now." Eben Bloch appeared through the smoke and ash, the gun raised and pointed at Unger. His face and clothes and hair were black with soot, and his broken arm rested in a sling, but he walked on his own. Aaron came running through beside him, holding out a blood-stained knife.

"You're too late!" cried Unger.

Eben lunged at Unger before Aaron could stop him. The two elderly men tumbled to the ground, and the gun went off.

The smell of the corn and the feel of the stalks brushing against her skin were so real. Reggie knew she was still in the fearscape, but the sea of soft yellows, greens, and oranges was undeniably tranquil. With every step she took forward, the softness of the cornfield lowered her adrenaline. Her heartbeat, racing since the moment she slipped off the doorframe in the school hallway, slowed enough for her to breathe deep and calm. She could walk and walk amid the gentle cornstalks forever.

And the moment that thought penetrated her mind, Reggie wondered if that was what the Vour had wanted when it constructed this level of Quinn's fearscape.

She did a slow turn inside the corn, and every degree of her surroundings looked identical. Seven ears of corn grew from each stalk, three on the left and four on the right. Each had the same number of green blades, reached the exact same height, and stood equidistant from one another. An anxious throb pulsed in her chest.

"Fight it, Reggie," she said aloud. "It wants you to freak out. Don't let it."

She pushed forward.

"Walk straight. And keep going."

Growing up in a rural community like Cutter's Wedge, children learned certain things at an early age, and Reggie knew the drill. Don't cross bridges when the wash gets high, don't touch a farmer's tractor without permission, and never panic if you've gotten turned around playing in a cornfield.

If you go too deep and lose your direction, walk a straight line until you come out on the other end. Even if you're miles from where you started, you'll never truly be lost.

She figured scared, little Quinn knew the drill, too.

The shadows in the corn grew darker and the air colder as she continued straight ahead. Surely, there was something menacing on the way, but what choice did she have? There was no turning back.

At last the patterns of some of the stalks changed, but just barely. However, Reggie had been inside long enough to pick up the subtle differences: four ears on the left, three on the right. The misfit stalks led her in a zigzag trail to a small clearing.

A crude scarecrow sagged upon a wooden pole, tufts of dried straw sticking out of a blue-black checkered flannel shirt and old, faded jeans. The thing did not move, but Reggie approached with caution, hunching over to look under the wide-brimmed sunhat and see the hidden face beneath.

For a brief moment, her thoughts retreated to the story of Jeremiah; it was one of the first she'd read in the old journal that introduced her to the Vours. The boy's drunken father had strung him up on a cross in a cornfield as punishment decades ago. His terror out in the night had summoned a Vour on Sorry Night, and his little sister, Macie, could not save him. When Jeremiah grew old and sick from cancer, Macie, then an old woman herself, locked him in a cell in her basement and waited for him to die. When he finally did, the Vour was trapped.

Until Reggie let it out years later and destroyed it. She then devoured its remains herself and unleashed an inexplicable power inside her. It all seemed like a horrible nightmare, but it had happened. And now she stood in a cornfield not unlike the one where Jeremiah had been sacrificed to the dark.

Reggie pulled an ear off the closest stalk and threw it. The corn struck the scarecrow's hat and knocked it off. The soft pumpkin head beneath toppled to the ground with a squishy thump.

But nothing else happened.

The head didn't spew forth maggots that grew into raging

demons; the cornstalks didn't uproot and attack her. Just an eerie and dead silence hung all around.

Reggie picked up the head and stared through the carved eyes. Something was inside.

Reggie reached her hand into the opening on top of the pumpkin and pulled out a couple of wrinkled pumpkin seeds with a few strands of dried pulp.

And a homemade baseball card.

She examined it. The grainy photo of a little boy had been taped to construction paper, and a hand-drawn banner decorated the bottom. There was a name written with a royal blue marker.

3B — Kenny Cullens.

Why did the name sound familiar?

Reggie flipped the card over and found more handwritten information filled out inside carefully penciled boxes: batting average, home runs, slugging percentage, stolen bases, put-outs, fielding percentage.

At the bottom was a small section that said the one thing Reggie needed.

Best Friend: Quinn Waters.

A bread crumb.

He had been here. And she was getting closer. She knew that now. But he was hidden from her.

Reggie tucked the card into her pocket, placed the pumpkin head back on the scarecrow, and continued to follow the trail of odd stalks, hopeful that she'd soon find her way out.

Faster and faster she moved, now able to more easily distinguish the subtly different stalks. She saw the field open again and stepped into another clearing.

No, not another clearing. The same one.

But one element had changed.

The scarecrow was gone.

Finding the baseball card, discovering the bread crumb — she had awakened yet another monster born of Quinn's deepest fears. And the trail she'd followed, believing that she'd discovered the secret of the corn, had only led her back to where she'd been.

So this time Reggie closed her eyes and just walked. The corn, once soft and lush against her face, now felt rough and harsh like sandpaper. The blades grated her cheeks and poked at her throat, slicing shallowly into her skin. But she kept walking, and she kept her eyes shut. No false patterns, no rising or setting false sun in a false sky, no psychic pain would alter her step.

"Feel for him," Reggie said aloud. "Reach. He's out there."

Straw crunched and the quiet brush of flannel seemed to whisper behind her.

"Look."

A voice, thin and raspy.

"Look . . . at . . . me . . ."

The scarecrow.

She squeezed her eyes shut and walked.

"Wrong way."

It was right behind her.

"Lost . . . so lost . . ."

Straight. Keeping going straight.

Reggie could sense the thing right over her shoulder. She smelled the straw and the scent of pumpkin. But she did not run and did not veer. Straight. If you walk straight through a cornfield, you will never truly be lost.

"You are mine."

A single blade of straw touched the back of her bare neck and streaked slowly down between her shoulder blades.

"Never get out."

The air grew warmer. Like sun on her face.

"No . . ."

The voice was louder now, bitter.

"Look at me!"

She was nearly out, but she did not dare look until her face and hands sensed no corn stalks around her. And then she slowly opened her eyes. She stood before a ladder on the side of a massive grain silo in the middle of a peaceful and deserted farm. She still sensed the scarecrow behind her, but now she heard something else — a distant sound in the sky coming closer.

The fluttering of many wings.

"You shouldn't have followed me out here." Reggie saw its horrific shadow stretched out across the side of the silo, large and jagged, but she did not turn around.

"Why is that?"

"Crows love pumpkin seeds."

The birds descended.

Reggie gripped the ladder and scrambled up as feathers, beaks, and talons flew down around her. She threw herself through the opening near the top of the silo, still refusing to look back, but she heard freakish squawks and the thrashing of straw below her.

Once inside, she was instantly buried in grain and dust. Some unseen valve had been opened, sucking her down through another portal, grain choking her and filling her lungs . . .

. . . she awoke upside-down, trapped between two crumpled bench seats at the rear of a flipped over, incinerated yellow school bus. The frame of the vehicle had been crushed, the windows had been blown out, the seats melted. Baseball caps and cleats littered the smoldering ceiling, now the floor. She smelled burnt hair and old bubble gum.

Reggie wriggled out of the seats and dropped to the roof of the bus with a painful thud. She gathered herself and climbed out of a window.

Spatters of dried blood marked the asphalt and dirt. Ash blew down the sidewalk, spiraling around piles of broken glass and smoldering mounds of rubber. This was the scene of a horrible traffic accident.

Reggie recognized the geography of old town Cutter's Wedge, a section of town that only a decade ago bustled with factories and shops. When hard times had hit, many businesses went under or moved from town. It had become a haunted-looking place.

Her heart filled with dread. She found no bodies here, no survivors, nothing alive. Nothing about this place hinted that Quinn had been here or even lingered nearby.

It struck her that she knew nothing about the true Quinn, about who he was as a human being. Had she moved too hastily through this fearscape? Missed clues?

She'd recovered only a single token — the baseball card — from the layers of the fearscape, just one psychic bread crumb. Was she moving closer to the young boy imprisoned here?

The time she'd spent with the Vour Quinn had proved to be nothing but a great deception. She'd been a fool out there. So why not in here, too? She didn't know Quinn. She knew only the monster.

And she'd *allied* herself with it. *Trusted* it.

And she'd let herself be tricked by it — again and again and again. She was lost. Sooty air burned her throat as she wandered into the center of the deserted street.

"Quinn, where are you? I don't know what to do." She sat in the dirt, the smell of burning rubber and oil filling her lungs. "I don't know how to find you. Help me."

A soft breeze carrying the scent of bubble gum blew gently in Reggie's face.

"Quinn?"

Nothing.

"Quinn? Can you hear me? I'm here to take you home."

A soft, squishing sound behind her.

She whipped around.

Nothing.

"Quinn? Please. Let me take you home."

The squishing sound started again, and then Reggie saw it. Like a water snake skirting slowly across the surface of a pond, the moist, grayish length of thin rope unfurled and slid across the dusty ground toward her. She waited in silence for it to reach her.

Entrails.

But whose?

Reggie reached out and took gentle hold of the intestine. It slithered and wrapped around her hand and tugged. She stood up and followed.

It wound back around the burning cars, back through the overturned bus, and off into a dark corner of the fearscape until it reached the edge of a steep precipice. There, it unwound itself from her hand and retracted out of sight down the side of the cliff.

Down.

It beckoned her.

Turning her back to the black chasm, Reggie dropped to her knees. Then she slid backward down the cliff with only the sense of touch to guide her on the dangerous descent.

Aaron ran to Eben's side, but the old man shooed him off.

"The wires. Disconnect her from the rest of them," he grunted.

Aaron nodded and flew back to Reggie. She lay so calmly on the stone slab amid the chaos around her. The wires and tubes attached to the needle throbbed with electricity; Aaron made sure he was grasping the plastic hilt of the knife, then sliced through the wires, severing the connection with the rest of the bodies in the room.

There was a flash of light and all the monitors shorted out.

The human bodies lay twitching on their slabs, and Aaron felt a tremendous grief. All this pointless death.

"No!" shouted Unger.

The doctor was bleeding from the shoulder where he had been shot, but he had managed to crawl a few feet away from Eben, who lay gasping and wheezing on the ground.

Aaron saw that Reggie's and Quinn's hands were tied together. Even with all the danger surrounding them, he couldn't risk separating them. Reggie was still in the fearscape, and rupturing contact now could trap her inside a living nightmare forever.

22

Two boys existed in dark solitude on a small stony outcrop hundreds of feet down the side of the cliff. One of them was splayed out, his tiny body broken and twisted in a tortuous heap on the rocks. His eyes were closed, and his head rested in the lap of the other boy. Reggie instantly recognized them both.

"Hi, Quinn."

He did not look at her. He stared out into the swirl of gray in the vast sky beyond the mountainside.

"Hello," he said, as if he'd been expecting her for some time.

Reggie knelt down next to them.

Kenny's entire abdomen had been slashed open by something harsh and jagged. Flies buzzed around the gaping wound, and thousands of maggots undulated inside the split skin. The entrails that had guided Reggie downward had coiled back inside the boy's horribly damaged body. But he wasn't dead. His breath was shallow and ragged, but he remained alive.

"I'm here to take you home," Reggie said.

"Don't want to go," Quinn answered.

"You heard me. You answered. You brought me here."

"No. It wasn't me." Quinn shook his head. "It was him."

"You don't want to leave?"

"Can't. Have to stay."

Reggie looked at the baseball card and her heart wanted to break. Something truly tragic had happened to this boy, and Quinn had witnessed it. His guilt was deep, and here on this tiny cliff it stagnated. Spoiled. Grew rank in the air.

"Kenny was your best friend, wasn't he?" Reggie inched closer, but Quinn shuffled nearer to the cliff's edge, dragging the comatose boy with him.

"Still is," Quinn said defiantly.

"I'm sorry. *Is* your best friend." Reggie scanned the stats on the card. "Third baseman, right? Hot corner. Tough position."

"Yeah."

"Did he really hit thirty-seven home runs?"

Quinn let out a small laugh. "No. We just made those up. But he would have someday. I bet he would have."

"Would have . . . if what?" Reggie asked. She poised herself to leap if Quinn tried to take himself over the edge.

"If this didn't happen." Quinn touched Kenny's stomach, brushing off maggots and shooing flies. But the maggots only returned in greater numbers and the flies settled back down on the wounds. The effort was a tired and defeated one. The boy had sat on this cliff for years, Reggie realized, holding his dying friend and waiting. Just waiting.

The Vour kept the nightmare alive, having found the one thing that would keep Quinn forever paralyzed and unable to fight. Seeing him here, lost and hopeless, reminded Reggie of the moment she had discovered Henry in the cellar of the department store in his fearscape. He'd behaved much the same way. So had Keech, literally trapped in a more terrible version of himself.

Quinn was shackled by his own guilt and fear. No need for a lock and key anymore, not when he'd long given up. The only way to save Quinn now was for Quinn to save himself.

"Tell me what happened." Reggie sat down and crossed her legs. "What happened in the bus?"

Quinn turned to Reggie. His eyes were glazed and dim from years of staring into nothingness.

"We didn't mean it," he said sadly. "It was just for fun."

A fly crawled across Quinn's left eyeball, but he didn't notice. It buzzed there for a moment and then flew away.

"I would always bring packs of gum, enough for everyone on the team. And sometimes on the way back from games we'd get into gum fights. Nothing bad, but Coach and the bus driver told us not to. One time after a game in Wennemack, Kenny dared me."

"Dared you to what?"

"To throw gum at the bus driver. He said he'd give me his Mayers *rookie* card if I did it. I said no at first. But Damen and Greg wanted me to do it, too. They chewed up their gum and made it into a big, sticky wad. And they dared me to throw it. I didn't mean for anything bad to happen —"

Quinn choked up and looked away.

"He got so mad. It stuck in his hair and he started yelling. And the bus swerved when he turned around and screamed at us. I was looking at his red face and trying to hide behind my seat when the whole bus went upside down. I woke up on the roof of the bus. I was crying and holding my head. Other kids were crying, too. And Greg was bleeding out of his nose and screaming. But Kenny wasn't in the bus."

"Where was he?"

Quinn didn't answer.

"Did you find him?"

"Yeah."

"Where?"

"Outside. He got thrown out the window." Quinn's voice shook. "He got cut all open. I could see his insides."

"You found him like this." Reggie brushed Kenny's cold cheek with her hand. Quinn pulled him away.

"Don't touch him. I don't want him to die."

"Quinn?" Reggie touched Quinn's hair. He had the same soft locks as a young boy. "Quinn, I need you to hear me. And I want you to answer me. Please. Did Kenny die?"

Quinn moaned and refused to look at Reggie or the dying boy in his lap. The entrails slithered out of Kenny's stomach and grabbed hold of Reggie's arm. They squeezed hard as she tried to pull away. They squirmed up her arm and around her neck as she fought to rip them off.

A young Quinn had been consumed by an overwhelming fear that he'd caused his best friend's death. The Vour knew it. And it was silencing Reggie before she helped Quinn forgive himself.

"Quinn! Please!"

The boy turned to her, his eyes vacant.

"You shouldn't have come here," he said.

The baseball card fell from Reggie's hand as she struggled and landed on the open wound in Kenny's midsection. A broken, pale hand reached inside and pulled it out. Quinn stared at the photo.

"What happened to me?" Kenny moaned.

"You're hurt, Kenny," Quinn said. "You're hurt real bad. But I'm going to stay here until you get better."

"I don't want to die, Quinn," the boy wheezed.

"You won't die. I'm your best friend, Kenny. I won't let you."

The entrails tightened on Reggie's throat. She watched wide-eyed as Quinn and Kenny spoke, both of them — all of this — bizarre figments of a world inside Quinn's childhood psyche.

"Don't leave me, Quinn."

"I won't, Kenny. Not ever."

The intestine grew, wrapping around and around Reggie, pinning her arms to her sides so she couldn't struggle.

"Quinn," she choked. "That's not . . . your friend . . ." The entrails pulled Reggie toward the edge of the cliff. She wriggled fiercely, but the ropy organ was as strong as an iron cable.

Quinn bent down over his friend, the Vour, shielding him.

"Would Kenny want this for you?" Reggie cried.

"I don't know," Quinn said.

"Do you know where you are?"

"Shut her up, Quinn," Kenny snapped.

The intestine tightened, but she battled against it. "I've been trying to reach you and save you, Quinn! The bear. The insect-boy. The scarecrow. I've fought them all to find you! But only you can defeat this one! This is your fight — I can't do it for you!"

Quinn looked from her to Kenny, confused.

"I can't fight Kenny," Quinn pleaded. "He's —"

"It isn't your friend! It's the monster!"

"She doesn't belong here!" the Vour hissed. "Get rid of her. Then it will be the two of us again."

The entrails pulled Reggie another foot closer to the drop-off.

"Would Kenny want you to kill?" Reggie asked.

"No . . ."

"Look at that thing. Does it really look like your friend?"

Quinn stared at the broken boy's face, and it flashed and crackled like a bad circuit, giving Quinn glimpses of the bear, the insect-boy, the scarecrow.

"You're not him . . ."

The intestine surged up around Reggie's jaw before she could close her mouth and gagged her. She moaned and tried to spit it out; it tasted of slimy raw meat caked in rust and dirt. But it slithered tighter and she could not speak anymore. Her heels hung an inch over the edge of the abyss, but Quinn was staring down at the boy. The skin on his face melted away to reveal a gray skull.

"You're not Kenny," Quinn breathed. Then he jumped up. "You're not Kenny at all. Let go of her!" Quinn blinked. "Let go of me!"

The boy on the ground burst into a hive of smoke particles that darted around Quinn like bees. He swatted at them furiously.

"Go away!" he yelled. *"Go away!"*

His breath blew out of his mouth like a jet of wind, and it swept the smoke away until it disappeared into the ether. The intestines that bound Reggie slackened, released, and then vanished.

The landscape around them faded away, replaced with empty whiteness. Ahead of them a baseball dugout appeared, a strange, solitary opening in the vacant halls of Quinn's fearscape.

"That's the way home," Reggie said.

"What is this place?" Quinn asked. "Is it real? It feels real."

"I wish I knew for sure," Reggie said. "Part of it is in our minds, I think. But our minds are powerful things."

Reggie felt relief wash over her. Quinn was almost free. But then he pointed above them.

"What's that?" he asked. A tremble had crept back into his voice. Reggie looked up, but she could see only the whiteness all around them.

"What's what?"

"That."

"Quinn, I don't see anything."

"A black spiral, like a road. Far off. You can't see it?"

Reggie shook her head. Quinn's eyes sparked with worry.

"It's okay," Reggie said hastily. "This is the way out."

As she stepped down inside the dugout behind Quinn, Reggie chanced one more look back. But there was only white, empty space.

What had the boy seen?

23

A huge plume of smoke erupted from Quinn's body; it seemed to flow out of every pore, and a ghastly face formed in its roils. It rushed at Aaron, and he closed his eyes tightly as it broke apart over his skin. Then it was gone.

Reggie lay still, but her breathing was even. Aaron cringed at the sight of her. Half her skull had been shaved, and electrodes were glued to her scalp. He examined the needle sticking out of her forehead. He was afraid that if he pulled it out, it might do irreparable damage to her brain, but they all had to get out of here soon before the whole place caved in.

Gripping the needle with his thumb and forefinger, Aaron gingerly slid it out of Reggie's head. He had to pull harder than he would have liked, since it had pierced the bone, but finally he managed to extricate it. Moments later, Reggie shifted on the slab. Her eyes fluttered open.

"Reggie?"

She tried to move, but her limbs were numb.

"Are you back?"

"Yeah," Reggie murmured. "Good to see you."

"We gotta go."

He undid the cords around her wrists and the straps on her ankles. She grabbed him for support, and he helped her stand. She wobbled for a second, then took a step forward. The paralysis was beginning to wear off.

"Eben." She dropped to the old man's side. He looked up at her, black drool dripping from his lips. "We need to get you out of here."

Quinn started to awaken.

"Hold still," Aaron said, removing the needle from his head like he had from Reggie's. Quinn shuddered but stayed silent. His eyes were dazed, not registering his surroundings. Aaron noted that the black scars on his cheek seemed to be fading away already.

Another tremor rocked the chamber.

Aaron grabbed Quinn's arm and threw it around his shoulder, hoisting the boy to his feet. He dragged him toward the cave exit where the lucky Vours had managed to escape.

"This way!" he shouted back at Reggie, who had helped Eben up and was now supporting him forward.

"Hold your breath," she said to the old man as the smoke billowed around them.

They reached a place where the fallen dirt formed a ramp up into the open forest. Aaron and Reggie struggled with their charges, and Reggie felt especially weak. Adrenaline alone pushed her through. Finally they were up and out of the inferno; a warm summer breeze tickled their skin, and the dark sky above was giving way to the solstice dawn.

In the fiery trenches below, they did not notice Dr. Unger fade back into the shadows at the other end of the cavern and escape into the underground tunnels. He smiled to himself, for he had seen something the others had not.

He had seen where the essence of Quinn's Vour had gone when it had left the boy's body, and he found it very interesting.

———

Leaderless, the Vours had scattered into the woods.

"Come on," said Aaron, leading the way. "I saw where you parked Machen's car. I think we should drive that one back, since it's more borrowed than stolen."

"Stolen?" Reggie asked. Aaron shook his head.

They had only stumbled along a short distance before Eben collapsed in a horrid coughing fit. He bent forward on his hands and knees, hacking black phlegm into the dirt. The sound was so awful Reggie thought his throat might crack open. She knelt beside him and patted his back tenderly. Aaron let Quinn sink to the ground and joined Reggie by Eben's side.

Finally his coughs subsided, and he sat back, resting against a tree. His breaths came in ragged starts, and he closed his eyes.

"We have to keep going," Reggie said gently. "The cops'll be here soon. We'll get you back to the hospital right away, Eben."

A smile played about Eben's lips, and he shook his head.

"No more hospitals for me." He opened his eyes and looked around. The sun was just peeking through the trees, a candle atop a pink icing sky. "No, I think this is the perfect place."

"The perfect place for what?" Reggie asked anxiously.

Eben turned his kind gaze on her. He took her hand.

"Regina, my body has turned over more years than is possibly good for anyone. So many I stopped counting, in fact. I've been kept alive by a poison that devoured me. But I don't regret it, because these last few years brought me to you. You're a miracle, Regina Halloway, and I never saw many miracles, though I've been looking for over a century."

The tears welled in Reggie's eyes.

"Eben, I'm sorry I was so angry. It was stupid — I didn't mean any of the horrible things I said."

"I wouldn't blame you if you did. Sometimes we old folk lose our wits. I was wrong not to tell you the truth long ago." His voice was faltering, but he gazed eagerly at Reggie. "Your heart gives you your power, Regina," he murmured. "Follow it, fight with it, and you cannot be defeated."

With his last strength he squeezed her hand, then his eyes closed, and his head slumped to the side.

"Goodbye, Eben." Reggie threw her arms around his neck and sobbed quietly into his shoulder. She heard his feeble heartbeat slow and then stop altogether.

Aaron stood above them both, tears sloping down his cheeks. The sun had risen another half a foot, and in the distance he could make out the sound of sirens. He touched Reggie lightly on the shoulder.

"Come on, Reg. We've got to go."

Reggie nodded and wiped her eyes. She kissed Eben's forehead, then rose to her feet. She and Aaron helped Quinn the rest of the way to the car, and soon they were on the road to home, passing a series of police cruisers on their way.

Reggie had finally gotten a look at herself in the side mirror of the sedan. The vision was shocking — a hole in the middle of her forehead, all the hair on the left half of her head shaved completely off, the rest a dark tangle. Her scalp riddled with welts from the electrodes. She ran her fingers along the bald side of her head.

Aaron grabbed her hand.

"It'll grow back."

He parked the car on an isolated cul-de-sac near Reggie's house. Quinn had fallen into a deep sleep, his breathing slow and even. Aaron and Reggie stood beside the BMW's rear door and looked in at him. Reggie reached through the open window and found Quinn's weak and fluttering pulse. He stirred, but didn't wake.

"I think he's just exhausted," Aaron said.

"It might be worse than that."

"Well, we can't take him to the ER in town, and I don't want to risk any local phone calls," Aaron said. "I'll drive him to Boston."

"That's over two hours away. And we can't just dump him in the city —"

"I know, Reg." Aaron sighed. "I'll bring him by a homeless clinic or a shelter, then call in a report to the cops that he's there."

"What about the car?"

"Park it in the school lot? Look, I'll take care of it. Right now, you need to go home. Get cleaned up. Check in on Henry."

She nodded and hugged him before he clambered back in the car.

"Aaron?"

"Yes?"

"I'm sorry . . . about everything. I was horrible, and so stupid."

"Pretty much, yeah."

"Thank you. For saving my life. Again."

Aaron grinned at her.

"I'm getting pretty good at it, aren't I? I'll call you tomorrow, okay? Try to get some sleep."

The car sped away, kicking up a cloud of dust. The morning was already getting hot and sticky against her skin. Sparrows and magpies argued in the brush. She needed to get home.

Reggie cut through the woods and came out in her backyard. Treading stealthily, she came up onto the deck and opened the sliding glass door. Unlocked, thank God. She entered and closed it behind her without making a sound. With any luck, Dad was still asleep. She definitely needed to do something about her appearance. Maybe he hadn't even noticed she was gone.

She tiptoed across the kitchen and out into the hall toward the stairs. But as she passed the living room Dad called out to her.

"Reggie."

He was sitting alone on the couch in the dim light. Reggie had no choice but to go to him.

"Have you been here all night?" she asked meekly.

"I have." His eyes widened at the sight of his daughter, and he jumped to his feet. "Reggie — oh my God! Your head — what happened to you? Are you hurt?"

Reggie felt so tired, so weary. She had no more lies left in her, no covers. She sank onto the sofa next to her father, and she could not stop the tears.

Dad put his arms around her.

"Please, Reggie. Did someone do this to you?"

She nodded, sniffling.

"Tell me. Whatever it is, we'll get through it together."

Reggie hesitated only a moment more, then launched into the story of the Vours, from the first time she'd picked up Macie's journal to Eben's death less than an hour ago. Dad listened attentively, nodding and only asking the occasional question as she spun the tale of Sorry Night and told him the dark side of Cutter's Wedge. It all came out in a rush, a torrent of words — but it felt so good to finally speak the truth that she couldn't stop.

Dad was silent for several minutes when she had finished. "So Mr. Bloch . . . he's dead?"

Reggie's face constricted. "Yes."

"And Henry?"

"I think he's going to be okay, Dad. He's strong."

"He sure is. And so are you."

"I don't know what's going to happen next," Reggie said. "They'll come after me again. This isn't finished. I don't know how to keep fighting —"

Dad pulled Reggie into a hug and held her tightly.

"Oh, Reggie. Don't you know that I'll help you fight?"

They stayed like that for a bit, and Reggie felt like she was five years old again, running to her father after waking from a nightmare. This nightmare wasn't over, she knew, but maybe they could all make it through it, together.

EPILOGUE

Reggie slept the entire day. Dad had helped her up to bed and checked on her throughout the day, and finally near dusk brought a tray of food up to her room. The sight of his daughter lying there, so scarred and ravaged, nearly broke him. He sat down on her bed, and Reggie's eyes fluttered open.

"Hey, kiddo. I thought you should eat something. I brought you some soup."

Reggie smiled at him and sat up, taking the tray. The comforting aroma of steaming chicken noodle soup filled her nostrils.

"Did you get a good sleep?" Dad asked.

Reggie nodded. "Where's Henry?"

"He's playing at a friend's." Dad fell silent, though it looked like there was more he wanted to say.

"Dad, what is it?"

"Reggie, I'm just — I'm just so sorry. This is all my fault. I had no idea what was going on."

"No, it's not your fault. You can't feel bad — the Vours have most people fooled."

Dad kneaded his hands together.

"I don't want you to worry. We're going to get you the help you need."

Reggie took a bite of soup and stared at him questioningly.

"What do you mean?"

"I know you took my sleeping pills, Reg," Dad said, taking her hand. "And, God, look at your wrists. You've been cutting yourself. And this thing with your hair. You've been mutilating yourself to get my attention. I'm so sorry I didn't see it earlier, Reggie. I was so preoccupied with Henry, no wonder you acted out."

Reggie pulled her hand away from her father.

"Dad, no, I told you. Those pills were for Quinn. And my wrists — that's from the cord that Dr. Unger tied them with. The Vours are real! Daddy, you have to believe me!"

"I believe that you believe it," Dad said. "We're going to get you better, Reggie, trust me."

He glanced at the door, and Reggie followed his gaze. A man and a woman in Thornwood uniforms stood just outside her bedroom. They smiled pleasantly, and Reggie felt her insides churn.

"No! No!" She jumped up, spilling the soup all over the bed. Her father got hold of her in his strong arms and held her close.

"It's going to be okay, baby girl. It's going to be okay. I told you, I'm going to help you fight this."

Reggie bucked and thrashed against him, and the hospital staffers came forward. The woman held out a syringe.

"This will calm you down, dear." As Dad held Reggie, the woman plunged the needle into her arm.

Reggie felt the medicine surge through her and her limbs became numb. She looked searchingly at her father.

"Please don't do this."

"I know you'll hate me for a while, but we need to get you healthy," said Dad. His voice sounded like it was coming from another room.

Reggie went limp as the orderlies got her downstairs and onto a stretcher. They rolled her out to an ambulance parked in the driveway. She moaned and screamed incoherently, her cries disturbing the quiet evening street. A neighbor out for a jog eyed them suspiciously, and a homeless-looking man with ripped clothing and whitish blond hair stumbled down the sidewalk toward them.

"Don't worry, she's okay," Dad called to the neighbor. He peered at the homeless man as he staggered by. He wore a strange look of horror on his face, and Dad saw that he had a red gash across his throat. "She's fine, buddy. Keep moving."

Reggie's unfocused eyes fell on the man. She knew him. How did she know him? Then it hit her.

"Help me!" she groaned. "Mach —"

But before she could say any more, they loaded her inside the ambulance. Her father kissed her, and they slammed the doors shut. Tinted windows lit the ambulance with steely gray light, and an IV bag swayed over her head as they backed out onto the road. Through the window she thought she saw the man pull out a cell phone; he stared anxiously after the ambulance as it drove away.

"The Tracers," Reggie rasped with the last of her energy. "They know. Machen knows. Aaron will know. They'll come for me."

"Try to relax," the man said. He bent over her with another syringe. Reggie fought to keep her eyes open and saw him empty a hypodermic filled with swirling black liquid into her arm. It felt cold and filthy in her veins.

Somebody help me! her mind screamed, but her lips wouldn't form the words.

"There, there," cooed the woman. "It's just a little shot. What are you afraid of?"

The fear continues in BOOK 3 of

THE DEVOURING

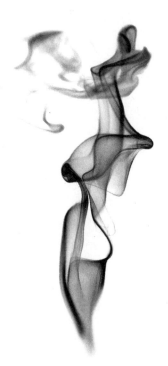

COMING FALL 2010.

WHAT ARE YOU AFRAID OF?